RUMORS OF GLORY

Peter M. Wright

PublishAmerica
Baltimore

Hardcover 978-1-4560-7108-0
Softcover 978-1-4560-7107-3
PUBLISHED BY PUBLISHAMERICA, LLLP
www.publishamerica.com
Baltimore

Printed in the United States of America

Let us cross over the river and
rest under the shade of the trees.
—*Last words of*
Thomas 'Stonewall' Jackson

Yon 'Flanders Fields' are ravaged and sorry,
'cause bold men trust,
those rumors of glory.
—*anonymous*

To the California 100
(Company A, 2nd. Massachusetts Volunteer Cavalry)
California to Appomattox

ACKNOWLEDGEMENT

Many thanks to First Sergeant Gil Hogue and Captain Keith Bowles of the National Civil War Association for their technical advice on this book.

A huge thanks to Emelie Poisson who graciously allowed herself to be the model for Savannah Johnston in this story.

CHAPTER ONE

It was raining. It had been for nearly three days. The barn was chilly and damp. The cow and horse scent was there. The same smell as his father's barn. A young foal whinnied and stomped. He had been recently weaned from his mother. He didn't understand about where she had gone. He was hungry and lonely and he yearned for the warmth of his mother. Joshua Cole felt a strong kinship to the lonely foal. The rain was steady on the barn's shake roof and the ages old cedar allowed rain to drip through and puddle in the straw and on the pine flooring. Joshua huddled in the straw beneath a wool blanket, the one he'd stolen from the Conrad's hired hand's shack. He felt guilty about it, but more than that he felt pitiable. He had made a decision. And now because of his decision he couldn't go home, maybe never. He was hungry. His clothes were wet; his shoes had squished with each slogging step on his way to the Conrad farm. Now he lay in the straw cold and lonely and regretting his choice. He had lost the unusual determination and strength he had felt earlier upon leaving. In the morning, if possible, he would see Katie before he left and with any courage at all he would tell her he loved her and would come back for her when the war was over. Were eighteen too young to love? Was it too young to love a girl of sixteen? Would she wait for him? Would he survive? After all, would the United States Army accept him? Would they believe he was old enough? After all he was big for his age, man-sized some said. Big enough to eat hay, a neighbor jested one day after church.

Would he be allowed to serve in Army of the Potomac? Or any one of the big Union Armies? He would volunteer and serve wherever he was sent. The returning soldiers at the church had said that regular Union Army Soldiers were nothing but mercenaries and served for money whereas volunteers served for the cause and for love of country. They said that draftees from around the country deserted regularly because they didn't want to fight at all. They said some volunteers used fake names in order to collect the one hundred dollar bounty that was offered, then quickly deserted and volunteered again elsewhere to collect another bounty. But they also said that the volunteers were generally officered badly due to the political appointments of prominent men who had no military experience and often became brevet lieutenant colonels or even sometimes brigadier generals.

Would he be a coward? Run when the real fighting began? Cry and yell for his mother. Early on in the war he'd heard rumors of men badly wounded crying for their mothers, even crying in their death throes. Maybe he would miss his mother, Elizabeth Cole, but not that man Henry Cole who claimed to be his father but never did anything to indicate he really cared. Once he told Joshua that "You boy, was a God-damned accident twine your mother and me. You were never intended." Joshua remembered thinking, "Yeah, well I wouldn't have chosen you for a father either, if I'd had any choice in the matter."

The only attention Joshua Cole had ever gotten from his father was frequent beatings and the remaining scars from a horse whip easily and frequently snatched from a spike in the barn. Joshua had tossed that evil whip into the woods before leaving. He remembered the whip making his skin crawl as he carried it away. He'd quickly washed his hands in a brook to rid himself from the contact of that hated tool, a contact he'd felt all too often since his ninth or tenth year.

Joshua opened the army haversack, the one he'd found in the bushes along with a lot of other military stuff after more than a mile of Union Army troops had marched by the Cole farm. It had been a hotter-than-hell day, as he'd heard the soldiers complain while they'd tossed heaps of army gear aside to lighten their loads as the mounted officers yelled at the wastrels but without effect. No guns had been tossed aside, but hordes of overcoats littered the roadside, warmth that would eventually be sorely missed during the all too frequent Pennsylvania rains and bone-numbing cold. Joshua remembered spending hours combing the woods along the road when he was supposed to be splitting wood, hoping beyond hope to find a pistol or rifle, or even a bayonet. He had found a Union kepi and was even more pleased when he discovered that it was a near perfect fit. The hat was now safely stored away at the bottom of the army haversack he'd found in the bushes. He let himself dream about the day when he would wear a full Union uniform.

Being able to read, he had eagerly perused any newspaper he could get his hands on for news of the war, the War Between the States they were calling it, others called it the War of Rebellion, some said it was a civil war, whatever that meant. It didn't sound too civil after reading all the news of men being killed and maimed by the thousands. Rumor was that the Rebs were even burying their dead in big long trenches by the hundreds. Some of the soldiers at the church said that the Reb Army even buried some of their own still alive because they were too shot up to fix. Some said that the Rebs were southern heathens and blasphemous to the core. But Joshua's mother had told him that southerners where folks just like us and not to be believing those God-less ex-soldiers at the church. She'd said that some of them probably hadn't heard a shot fired in anger. Maybe some of them were deserters or slackers at the most. But Joshua continued to listen eagerly to their uncertain tales of the war.

Joshua Cole had read newspaper stories about the fierce battles taking place down in the Shenandoah Valley and how Stonewall Jackson's Army of Northern Virginia, called the Stonewall Brigade, had raised havoc with the Union Army's efforts to keep the Rebs out of the valley and from moving north toward the U.S. Capital. He'd read that Honest Abe was terrified that the Reb Army would over-take the Capitol and he'd be hung along with the rest of the Washington bureaucrats. But Joshua doubted that Abe Lincoln was afraid of Rebs, or anything else for that matter. After all, Abe Lincoln was a tough farm boy just like Joshua Cole.

Joshua had especially liked reading about the battle at Gettysburg that had taken place a year or two before and how a young colonel named Chamberlain, from somewhere up in Maine, had thoroughly whipped the Rebs on a hill called Little Round Top and how that victory had changed the course of the war. He had been intrigued by reports of some place called Devil's Den at Gettysburg where Reb snipers had shot at Union troops and how Union marksmen had shot them from far away at a couple hundred yards or so. And he'd read about the aftermath at Gettysburg and how hundreds of both Union and Confederate soldiers had been left dead and dying on the battlefield and how Union General Meade had gone off chasing Lee's trampled army and taking nearly all the medical staff and supplies with him. The newspapers reported that most of the dead and many of the wounded were still lying on the battlefield days or even weeks after the fight and how the local women-folks had stepped up and fed and treated the wounded as best they could. One paper called these women *Angels of the Battlefield.* However, at least two northern papers called the women traitors for caring for Rebs as well as Union soldiers and referred to them in one instance as *Devils in Petticoats.*

Union soldiers returning home after their initial enlistments were up, some wounded, of course, sat around the picnic area outside Reverend Black's First Baptist Church on Sundays and told fabulous stories of how they'd fought the Rebs and how glorious it was when they'd put them on the run or even when they knew for sure they'd killed one. One ex-infantryman had told the story of about how the Rebs were charging and he was loading his Springfield musket when a Reb was right on top of him and he'd had to fire without pulling the ram-rod out of the barrel. He'd told about how the ramrod had gone straight through the Reb and stuck in the leg of another one. He'd told about how after the battle he'd gone out and found the dead Rebs and retrieved his ram-rod from the body and how his first sergeant had commended him for his quick thinking and made sure he would get a second dram of whisky that night even though the whiskey rations were short, even nowhere to be found. Rumor was, he said, that most of the whiskey went to the officers as 'medicinal needs' and how that really angered the troops. He'd said that drunken officers on the field and even in battle were pretty regular stuff. He said the troops had often heard stories that U.S. Grant was often drunk in his tent. Some of the soldiers had nicknamed Grant, Usually Soaked Grant. But Joshua Cole didn't believe a word of that about General Grant. He would join the Union Army and do his part to put down the Rebellion and then come home, hopefully a hero, and not maimed, and with his army savings, thirteen dollars a month, marry Kathryn Hespeth and read for the law with Jerome Peabody, the town lawyer. Katie wanted to be a school teacher.

One thing that Joshua had heard was that those Secessionist Rebs had to be beaten, brought to their knees. He'd heard about some Union general named Sherman that swore he'd 'make them southerners howl' or something like that. The soldiers at the church had also claimed something about the war being about freeing the niggers, at least that was what they called those black slaves brought over from the jungle. One soldier who's right sleeve was empty, said that the war was about commerce. A war to make the arms manufacturers and food producers rich. He'd said he was glad that the army wouldn't have him back because he wasn't gonna die for no 'gal-damned store-keeper. Another soldier said he thought it was a damned-good idea making the 'niggers' slaves. He said that they mostly weren't as smart as mules. But Joshua remembered hearing the Reverend Black reading something in church that said 'all men were created equal' and then he said that we white folks shouldn't look down on folks of color and that no man has the right to enslave another. He said we've got to make Jesus our guidepost for life and that Jesus died for mankind, and that included folks of color, and then he added, "even if they ain't as smart as mules." Some folks in the congregation snickered aloud at that.

CHAPTER TWO

The Farm

Something had changed. Joshua Cole opened his eyes and lay there in the hay trying to figure out what it was. Then he mumbled aloud, "Rain has stopped." The horses were stomping there hooves, hungry and looking for water. Joshua panicked. He'd slept too long. The farmer could show up at any minute to feed the stock and milk the cows. He heard a noise and then saw a match flare in the early morning gloom of the barn. Then a lantern brightened and he could hear the farmer mumbling to himself. Joshua froze, daring not to breath. He was sure the farmer could hear his teeth chattering. He thought about making a run for the door. Was everything ruined now? He had the stolen wool blanket and the three dollars he'd taken from his father's chest of drawers.

"Shut-up horse," he heard the farmer say. "I'll feed ya soon as I can."

Then the farmer was silent. Unmoving. "Who's there?"

Joshua lay still, holding his breath.

"Quit stomp' in horse," the farmer yelled, "I cain't hear good. Who's there? Speak up for I grab my axe."

Joshua resolved he'd been caught and got to his feet slowly, feeling defeated and chilled to the bone. His head hurt and he itched from the hay.

"It's just me sir," he said. "Josh Cole."

The farmer raised the lantern and walked over to Joshua. "Why it is the Cole boy. What ya doing in my barn, boy? Ya'll in trouble? Ya'll didn't git that Katie girl in a family way did ya?" Then he snickered.

Joshua hesitated then decided to confess. "I'm on my way to join up with the United States Army. I had to sneak off else my Pa would 'a stopped me."

The farmer set the lantern down on a barrel-head, fished around in his coat and lit a corn-cob pipe, then crushed the match between his fingers. Joshua could feel him staring from beyond the arc of the lantern light.

"Lad," he said, "that's not a good idea. You're gonna get yourself kilt or damaged for keeps. Your daddy needs to know 'bout this?"

"No sir, he'd whip me if he knew 'bout it. He'd come after me."

"What is you ain't got no business joining the army. You better git on home 'fore your daddy catches up and whips the nonsense out of you."

Joshua stiffened. "No sir, I ain't going home. I'm joining the Army and doing my part to put down the Rebellion."

"You ain't old 'nuff. Besides your daddy needs your help on the farm. Now git 'fore I give you that lick 'in myself. Rebellion, bah! Ain't no problem of yours. Free' in them darkees is a bad idea."

"Ain't 'bout that," Joshua said, "it's something about breaking up the Union."

The farmer guff-offed. "Boy, you don't even know what a union is."

"May be," Joshua said, picking up the blanket and the haversack. He turned his back on the farmer and walked toward the door. He was aware he was shaking.

"I'm eighteen last month and I don't need my Pa's permission."

"Likely you cain't prove it to the army."

"I can," Joshua said.

"Jesus," the farmer said, "if' your bent on leaving ya'll need some food."

Joshua stopped and turned. The farmer waved his pipe.

"I don't need anything," Joshua said and turned.

"Boy, go on in the house and Ma will feed you. I'll be along. Tell her I sent you in."

An hour later with his belly full of flapjacks, eggs and ham, wearing a heavy coat, though thread-bare and too small, with his haversack crammed with berry jam and two loaves of bread, and a thick slice of cured ham, Joshua walked down the lane away from the farm, stopping to look back and feeling evermore lonely. The farmer and his wife were standing on the front porch watching him go. She was waving lightly and the farmer was shaking his head. Joshua gave a final wave and walked on, still not sure of himself and fairly regretting his decision to leave home and join the army. He longed to be with Katie Hespeth but knew he wouldn't see her again for a long time, if ever. The morning sun was partly breaking through the clouds and Joshua, warmed some by the light, felt that it was a good omen, because he had always known that he could be frightened and uncertain in the deep loneliness of night, but that it was always much easier to be brave in the morning's first light. It was always easier to be tough in the sunshine.

CHAPTER THREE

Camp Curtin

After getting off the train at Camp Curtin Joshua began to wonder if he had done the right thing. Camp Curtin near Harrisburg, Pennsylvania looked intimidating. Trainees were marching in long columns with sergeants wearing substantial stripes up and down the sleeves of there uniforms while screaming and cursing. Joshua was directed to a recruiting booth manned by the imposing figure of a soldier filling out forms and barking loudly as each volunteer stepped up to the table. Joshua took his place in the line as he was directed by a soldier who identified himself as Corporal Homan. He was not polite and his manner tended to prove he hated every volunteer in line. Joshua couldn't figure out why these soldiers appeared to detest every volunteer. After all, these recruits were there of their own free will volunteering to fight the Rebellion in the South.

Standing in line with 25 or 30 other volunteers Joshua began to look around and scrutinize his surroundings. He didn't like what he saw and was beginning to think that at this early hour he could be back on the farm feeding cows and chickens and anticipating his mother's routine unlimited breakfast of flap jacks, eggs and bacon. He began to think that maybe he should just walk away. He was broke. The train ride to Harrisburg had cost him the entire three dollars he had stolen from his father.

The fair had actually been four dollars but the station master, after learning he was on his way to volunteer, sold him at ticket for three dollar and kicked in the other dollar out of the goodness of his heart and his respect for the men volunteering to fight for the preservation of the Union.

"Step up, God damn it," the recruiting sergeant yelled.

Joshua Cole edge forward. The tall man in front of him looked old and weary, his clothes shoddy, dirty, and he smelled of whiskey. Unsteady he stood before the uniformed man who bore three stripes on his sleeve supporting a diamond in the V. Three stripes was mustached and chewing on the stub of a dead cigar. He looked tired, bored, and by the scowl on his face, ready to slug anyone who had the nerve to hesitate or not speak up when called on. This man is a leader, Joshua thought.

"Move on man, you're too old. Next, for God's-sake," he growled.

The whisky smelling man hesitated, "But..."

The sergeant motioned him away with a sweep of his hand. The whiskey smelling man staggered away, his head down and shoulders sloping. The sergeant stared at Joshua from beneath the bill of his cap. It's just like the kepi I found, Joshua thought.

Joshua inched forward. "Okay," he said.

The sergeant looked up for his paperwork. "What did you say?"

Joshua swallowed hard. "I...I said okay."

"Boy, I'm First Sergeant Dan Kelly and don't you ever say okay to me again or anywhere else in this God-damned army. Sir...you call me sir. You speak to me you say sir first and last."

"Okay...yes sir, Sergeant Sir."

The sergeant pulled out a new recruitment form and dipped his quill in the ink well. "Name?" Then stared at Joshua with great annoyance.

"Joshua Cole." Joshua found it difficult to get the words out.

Sergeant Kelly looked up. "You a slow learner, or what?"

Joshua swallowed hard. "Sir...Joshua Cole...sir."

Sergeant Kelly put his quill down and stared at Joshua. "How old are you?"

"Sir...18...sir."

"When were you born?"

"Sir...don't rightly know...Sir. Family bible burned and my folks are dead." Joshua hated lying and saying his mother was dead. He hoped he wasn't creating a bad omen. His father...oh well.

"Well, you're big enough. Even without a beard."

"Sir...?"

Sergeant Kelly ignored him. "You even shave yet?"

"Sir, yes Sir, nearly every day...Sir."

Sergeant Kelly kept scribbling on the form, and then looked up.

"Can you write your name?"

"Yes sir. I can write and read...some...sir."

Sergeant Kelly scowled. "Well ain't that sweet. You can God-damned read and write. Hell we might have to make you a general. Sign your name."

Joshua signed his name, his hands shaking so badly the writing was almost illegible.

Sergeant Kelly took the quill from Joshua's hand and slammed it down on the table. "Since the beginning of this war Camp Curtin has seen more than two hundred thousand recruits come through it and I damned well believe the quality of you so-called volunteers is getting damned poor. This here bunch is about the worse I've seen. Sometimes I think Abe Lincoln is scraping the bottom of the barrel these days."

18

Kelly pointed at a group of men standing in front of an army building with a sign above the door reading 'Quartermaster General.'

"Git over there General Cole and speak to that officer. He'll swear you in. This is your last chance to run. Once you're sworn in you're here for at least 3 years or for the duration of the war, or whichever comes first. Run off...and we'll have to shoot you, or hang you....now go."

Joshua hesitated. He didn't know whether to salute...or run.

Kelly looked up and scowled. "Go."

Joshua stood in a line of 20 or so men and boys. Next to him was a young man not more than Joshua's age. He looked scared and about ready to run. A lieutenant with two gold bars on his shoulders stood in front of the line reading from a list a soldier with two stripes on his sleeves had delivered to him from Sergeant Kelly's table.

The lieutenant handed the sheath of paper back to the corporal.

"Corporal Homan, spruce these men up a bit. They look bored with the United States Army. Can you inform them?"

The corporal stiffened and saluted. "Sir, I'd be more 'in happy to wake up these here farm boys." He turned and grinned at the nervous recruits.

"I'm getting out 'a here," the boy next to Joshua said.

Joshua looked at him and shook his head. "Don't you wanna help put down the Rebellion?"

"Well yeah, but these guys are treating us bad for nothing at all. We ain't even in the army yet."

"You with the mouth," the corporal yelled, "shut up, and all you toads come to attention."

The entire line of recruits did their best to stand at attention. They looked awful. The corporal walked up to the line and stood staring into Joshua's face. Joshua blinked and looked away. The corporal grinned.

"What's your name, boy?" The corporal was probably no more than three or four years older than Joshua.

"Joshua Cole…I mean Joshua Cole, sir."

"Why don't you run home to your momma?" the corporal said. "Looks to me like you still got the pot-rings on your butt."

The corporal moved down the line insulting every recruit and then ordering him to stand tall and criticizing his struggling efforts. Josh heard the boy next to him. "Let's git the hell out 'a here."

The corporal snapped around. "What did you say?"

The boy swallowed hard. "Nothing."

The corporal walked back to the boy. "What's your name, dog-mouth?"

"Bobby…Robert Jenkins."

"Robert Jenkins, sir," the corporal yelled, grabbing Jenkins' shirt front.

"Sir," Jenkins said his voice barely audible.

"You gotta middle name, Jenkins?"

"Lee, sir."

"Well I'll be damned," the corporal said. "We've got a Robert Lee. Damn, just like old Robert E. Lee, that Rebel General that'll soon git his southern ass whipped. Make him run like a rabbit. Ha, ha, ha. Rabbit E. Lee. God damned traitor what's he is. Sum-bitch decided to go south."

"Yes sir, "Jenkins said.

"What ya'll think 'bout that?" the corporal said, looking at Joshua.

"Sir, I think your right, sir. I understand he could 'a commanded the whole Union Army."

"What you want here in this army, Farm Boy?"

"Help whip the Rebels, sir."

The corporal walked over to Joshua and shoved his face into Joshua's.

"How you ever gonna do that, Farm Boy?"

Joshua tried to the look the corporal straight in the eyes. "By killing Rebs, sir. I guess."

The corporal eyes grew large and staring. "So you're a killer, huh Farm Boy?"

Joshua froze. "Yes sir, I guess I'm gonna have to be."

"What have ya'll kilt before, Farm Boy?"

"Chickens and such. Some deer and coon."

"Chicken ever shoot at you, Farm Boy?"

"Well, ah, 'course not, sir."

It began to rain lightly. Joshua and the others were still standing at a facade of attention. The corporal had backed off and stood behind the lieutenant as he read the swearing in oath. When he finished all but one of the recruits raised his right hand and said, "I do."

"Jesus," the corporal yelled. "What's wrong with you Robert E. Lee Jenkins? You turned into a leg case already? Hell, Farm Boy, your only a 3 year man. War will be over long before that. You cain't go home to momma already."

"Ah...ah...no. I'm just not sure anymore."

The lieutenant stepped up to Jenkins and stared into his face. "Why the hell you show up here, boy? Why'nt you git the hell out'a here 'cause we want men in this here army and not blubbering babes that can't make up their own minds. Go on home to momma."

"Say I do," Joshua whispered to Jenkins.

Robert Jenkins looked at Joshua. "You think I oaught'a?"

The corporal stepped up to Joshua. "What'd you say, Farm Boy?"

Jenkins attempted an awkward salute and suddenly yelled, "I do."

CHAPTER FOUR

Government Livery

The waiting was interminable. Joshua was soon to learn that this was typical army life; hurry up and wait. His group of newly sworn-in volunteers were quickly shuttled aside and ordered to stand tall and keep quiet. Joshua spent the time looking around and trying to familiarize himself with his new surroundings. Camp Curtin was immense, stretching outward for what seemed like miles. Rows upon rows of what the army called 'A' tents were lined up in neat rows and seemed to stretch out into infinity. At a safe distance behind the tents he made out what he thought to be the toilet area, or the latrine, as he heard soldiers shout as they hurried in that direction. Periodically as the wind change directions he realized he was right. No one dared comment on the stench.

More than an hour later they were marched into the quartermaster's building where stacks of uniforms and equipment crowded the floors and shelves. Long tables were piled with uniform components and rough looking low-quarter shoes. Uniformed soldiers stood behind the tables handing out, or actually throwing, uniforms and equipment at the recruits. Joshua soon learned that the low-quarter shoes were called brogans and the coat; a sack-coat, the hat; a kepi, or some called it a forage cap.

Joshua's coat was two large. It hung on his shoulders. He buttoned it with difficulty. The button holes were too small.

The other recruits were struggling with odds and ends of equipment that either were generally too big or too small.

"Excuse me sir, Sergeant sir."

Sergeant Kelly was in the quartermaster building supervising the issuing of uniforms and gear. He was puffing furiously on a cigar and helping toss equipment toward unsuspecting men.

"What," he yelled at Joshua?

"My coat is too big, sir."

Sergeant Kelly walked around the table to Joshua. "Well ain't that too bad. Now private, what's your name? This ain't no haberdashery, now is it?"

"Sir, no sir, but I wanna look good."

"Private, get back in line…look good? It'll take more than a coat to make you look good."

Joshua continued through the long line trying desperately to catch each piece of gear that was being thrown at him. He hastily pulled on a pair of sky-blue 5 button trouser that were easily two or three sizes too big. He struggled with a pair of suspenders, trying to get them hooked into the trousers and arranged properly over his shoulders. Then came rough black brogans that felt too small and confused Joshua when he noticed there was neither a right nor a left with both shoes appearing the same. He sat on the floor and laced them up. They hurt and he complained. Mistake! The corporal was back and he kicked Joshua on the leg while glaring down at him. Joshua desired to strike out at the corporal but held back.

"Back on your feet, Farm Boy."

Joshua clambered back to his feet in time to have a wooden toothbrush tossed at him. When Robert Jenkins, just behind Joshua, reached out for his, Sergeant Kelly pushed his hand away.

"May I have my toothbrush, sir?"

Sergeant Kelly shook his head. "Private, the army issues one toothbrush for every three soldiers. Decide who you wanna share with. And you only git to use it once every three days. Share it with two others."

Bobby Jenkins stood in astonishment. "Get moving," Kelly shouted.

Wearing the dark sack coat and trousers and hobbling in the too tight brogans, Joshua was ordered to 'quick-step' to the next building.

"Quick-step means faster than a duck," Corporal Homan yelled.

Joshua struggled to run with his arms loaded with the unfamiliar gear: haversack, eating utensils, leather belt with an assortment of pouches, new kepi, poncho, gum blanket, 4 button cotton shirt, bedroll and straps.

A sign above the door of the next building identified it as a United States Army Arsenal. An assortment of privates and corporals were handing out long barreled smoothbore muskets. Joshua accepted his in both hands and felt the grease still present on the metal and wood stock. He wiped his hands on his new trousers and then regretted it. A corporal stood staring at him and shaking his head. When each man in the line had received his musket Sergeant Kelly appeared and ordered them to fall in near the back of the building.

"Fall in what? "Jenkins whispered, giggling.

"I think it means to line up." Joshua said.

As they stood in a facade of a line Joshua stuck out his right hand to Jenkins. "I'm Josh Cole."

Jenkins took his hand. "Bobby Jenkins. Glad to meet'cha."

The corporal was too close. "Shut up over there, Farm Boys."

"I already hate him," Bobby Jenkins whispered.

Josh grinned and nodded. "Corporal thinks he's a general. Let's call him General Farm-boy."

General Farm-boy walked over to Joshua and Bobby Jenkins. "Again, I'm Corporal Homan and I've been in this army three years and I've been recruiting volunteers for six months now and you two are the worse of the lot. Now you horses asses, shut up."

Sergeant Kelly approached the line. He was holding a musket in his hands and ordered Homan to return to the quartermaster. Corporal Homan looked perplexed. "Yes sir, Sergeant." Homan walked away looking back over his shoulder. Sergeant Kelly was smiling slightly. He tossed a half-smoked cigar away and spit on the ground, then walked over to Joshua. "What is that you're holding in your hand private?" He studied Joshua with an amused smile.

Joshua swallowed hard. "A rifle, sir."

"Ain't no rifle, private."

"Yes sir, if you say so, sir."

Sergeant Kelly turned to one of the older recruits, a man of 30 years or so. "What do you say about that, private?"

"Ain't no rifle sir." The private smirked at Joshua. "Why isn't it?" "Because it's a smooth-bore, that's why." "That's right," Sergeant Kelly said. "These muskets have no grooves in the barrel. Grooves in the barrel cause a bullet to spin and give it better trajectory and distance. These here muskets will be replaced soon with rifles but in the meantime you gotta live with these here. They ain't much accurate beyond fifty or so yards so you gotta look the Rebs in the eyes before you shoot. And...shoot low if you can. Shoot where a man lives, in his balls, that is. Takes the fight out 'a them right quick."

A recruit raised his hand. Sergeant Kelly frowned. "What?"

"When'll we get 'a shoot'im?"

"You'll git to shoot them when I say so. I'm First Sergeant Daniel Kelly and I'll be helping train ya'll…if that's even possible. That's Lieutenant Wilson over there and we've got Captain Reynolds, Lieutenant Colonel Shaw, and Colonel Pickins. Ya'll have met Corporal Homan. You'll soon meet the other corporals and sergeants. Welcome to the 98th Pennsylvania Volunteers, this here shabby group will be Company A. God bless Abraham Lincoln."

Bobby Jenkins giggled, "Welcome to hell that's what it is."

Sergeant Kelly looked directly at Joshua and Bobby Jenkins. They both froze. "You privates like to talk?"

"No sir, we don't much," Joshua said.

Sergeant Kelly walked over to Joshua and stared into his face.

"Seems you've got too much spunk."

"Yes sir, I guess so, sir," Bobby Jenkins cut in.

"Well I'm going to this war with you two boys and I'm gonna keep an eye on the both of you. See how much spunk you got when the Rebs are firing a perfect storm of lead down your throats."

"I won't be afraid," Joshua said, trying to look Kelly strait on.

Sergeant Kelly stepped up close to Joshua. "What's your name?"

"Josh Cole, sir."

"And you?"

"Bobby…I mean Robert Jenkins."

Sergeant Kelly scowled. "Sir."

"Robert Jenkins, sir."

"Now you'll listen up," Sergeant Kelly said, "because I'm gonna tell you about this here regiment and about this here musket."

Joshua tried to size up Sergeant Kelly. Something deep inside him decided he liked Kelly. Kelly looked strong and fit in his uniform. The three strips on his sleeve supporting a diamond in the notch looked convincing. He thought how much he'd like to wear those stripes. Heck, even two stripes like General Farm-boy. Sergeant Kelly wasn't real tall but he was big, with broad shoulders and a deep chest. He stood ramrod straight and walked with a swinging gate that suggested power and self-confidence. Beneath his kepi great strands and ringlets of unruly coal black hair tried to escape the cap's clutch. He was clean shaven with the exception of a thick and massive walrus mustache that drooped far below the corners of his mouth. His vivid blue eyes were piercing and looked straight into you. "A man to ride the river with," Joshua's father would have said.

"Let's call him Old Blue," Bobby Jenkins whispered, "like my old Blue Tick hound dog at home."

Joshua nodded. "How about Sergeant Blue? He ain't old."

Sergeant Kelly looked up from his manipulation of the musket.

"Private Cole come over here. Seems you're overloaded with spunk. I'm gonna drill you in front of these recruits for a spell and see if' I can wear you down a bit."

Joshua stepped forward. "Yes sir."

"And Private Cole what was that you just called me?"

"…Ah, nothing Sir."

"Private Jenkins what'd Private Cole here just call me?"

Bobby Jenkins swallowed hard. "Ah…nothing sir. It was me."

Joshua turned to look at his new friend. He knew that Bobby was covering for him. Jenkins stared at his feet.

"Yeah and what was that you said, Private Jenkins?"

"Ah…Sergeant Blue, sir."

"And why would you be disrespectful to your very own first sergeant and call him something like that?"

Kelly sat the butt of the musket on the ground and stared at Jenkins. Kelly showed a slight crinkle at the corners of his eyes. Joshua thought that just maybe Sergeant Kelly was amused and suppressing a grin.

"Private?" Kelly said.

Bobby Jenkins kept staring at his own feet. No answer.

"Well," Sergeant Kelly said, "I think you boys need to spend more time with Corporal Homan. Is that what you'll want? Or would you prefer to learn something about this here musket?"

The entire line of recruits turned in unison to glare at Joshua and Bobby Jenkins. "Need their asses kicked," someone offered. Kelly turned and scowled toward the comment.

One of the older recruits yelled at Joshua and Robert. "Both you assholes shut up."

Now Sergeant Kelly grinned and stepped over to the recruit. "Why I think we've got corporal material here. Private, what's your name?"

"Davis sir. Jimmy...James Davis."

Sergeant Kelly's eyes grew big. "Well I hope to hell you ain't related to that southern symbol of manhood, old Jeff Davis."

"No sir, not that Reb President Davis."

"Well Private Davis you're gonna be my guidon in this here regiment and help keep these recruits in line. You know how to carry a flag? A company flag?"

Davis grinned. "I kin sure in the hell learn sir."

"However you should know that guidons are big targets in battle. The company flag is always something the Rebs like to shoot at."

"I'd be honored to fall beneath that flag," Davis said.

Davis looked at Joshua and Robert. He couldn't hide the smirk on his face.

"Oh my hero that Corporal Davis," Bobby Jenkins whispered, "and he knows how to carry a flag."

"Shut up," Joshua said. "He ain't no corporal."

Sergeant Kelly stood looking at Davis and nodding his head. He put a hand on Davis' shoulder and then turned away.

All the recruits watched with fascination as Sergeant Daniel Kelly explained the workings of the Model 1842 Springfield 69 caliber smooth bore musket. The musket was due to be replaced by rifles with far greater range and accuracy. Kelly deftly demonstrated how the black powder charge was poured down the muzzle and tamped in place by the ramrod along with the paper cartridge remains and lead ball to top it off, followed by a small copper percussion cap placed firmly on the nipple.

On the farm Joshua had been brought up to hunt with an aging flintlock musket that had been handed down from his grandfather who'd carried it home from his service in the War of 1812. In Joshua's eyes the Springfield Musket was the finest in weaponry he'd ever seen. His grandfather's flintlock musket involved the same method of loading but required the flash pan to be primed with black powder and for sure a high-quality flint stone secured in the hammer to spark the powder pan with a cloudy flash and sudden discharge. Joshua had become the family meat hunter at the age of 12 and had been unusually successful at keeping the household larder filled with deer meat, turkey, and partridge. To his dismay he'd been required to slaughter the farm animals, chickens, pigs, goats and cows with an ax or sledge hammer. "Saves ball and powder," his father preached. Joshua had long ago decided he didn't like killing animals but realized that it was necessary if he and his family wanted to endure. His dear mother had often repeated the bible's designation that "mankind shall hold domain over the animals and fishes." She'd always held that that is why God directed Noah to carry at least one pair of every animal aboard the Ark before the Big Flood so that mankind could eat meat and create beasts of burden and continue to reside on the face of the fine planet he had selflessly fashioned in just 7 days. His father had often commented, when out of earshot of his mother, that "my pious little wife has always been and always will be, a dyed-in-the-wool bible-thumper." His father attended church sporadically only to appease his wife and keep peace in the house-hold. He'd frequently maligned the Reverend Black by saying he was probably one of those men who held with men instead of women. Whatever that meant?

When Sergeant Kelly finished his preliminary instructions on the function of the musket he ordered the recruits to pick up their load of new army equipment and clothes and report to a tented bivouac area behind the arsenal building and line up in front of the first row of white canvas tents. Corporal Homan was back. He was accompanied by a private carting a heavy load of what appeared to be swords. Corporal Homan lifted one out of the cart and held it high. All eyes followed the instrument.

"This is a bayonet. The bayonet fits on the end of your musket and it is used to skewer the livers, or balls, of the first damned Reb you get close to. You will learn to 'fix bayonets' and you will learn to 'gut' your enemy with your bayonet... takes the fight out of them."

"I'll use mine on General Farm-boy the first chance I get," Bobby Jenkins whispered.

"You may get your chance," Joshua whispered, "he's staring at you."

"Private Farm-boy," Corporal Homan yelled, staring at Joshua," step out here."

"Ah shucks," Jenkins whispered, "he thinks it was you."

"I'm gonna kill you, Jenkins," Joshua whispered.

"Private Farm-boy despite my being a combat veteran and hearing hundreds of cannon fires and muskets I kin still hear good and I heard what you said. So...Private Farm-boy, fix this bayonet on the end of that musket and do your goodest to skewer me."

Joshua stood frozen. Homan handed him a bayonet off the cart. The corporal was grinning from ear to ear. Joshua fumbled with the bayonet. He looked at Homan. "Not too... sure, sir."

"The ring on the grip part of the bayonet fits over the end of the barrel."

Joshua slid the bayonet onto the musket barrel and then looked at Homan.

"Well?" Homan said, backing away from Joshua and snapping a bayonet to the end of his own musket.

Out of the corner of his eye Joshua saw Sergeant Kelly approaching.

"What's going on here Corporal?" Sergeant Kelly said.

"Ah...nothing Sergeant. Just train 'in these here farm boys."

"Corporal git back to the arsenal and help out there."

"But these here farm boys got big mouths," Homan protested.

Sergeant Kelly stared at Homan. "The arsenal."

Homan spun on his heel and disappeared through the back door of the arsenal. Joshua breathed easier.

"Git back in line Private Cole."

"Sir?"

"Back in line and don't kill Jenkins there with that bayonet."

Sergeant Kelly assigned numbered tents from a list and then ordered the recruits to report to their assigned quarters, dress in full gear, and fall back in line in five minutes. Groans emanated from the line of recruits with each one wondering in his own way, why he'd joined the army. Joshua was gratified to learn that he and Bobby Jenkins had been assigned the same tent, but his new friend would have to learn to keep his mouth shut. A serious discussion was in order.

While struggling with unfamiliar gear in the tent Joshua and Bobby heard the first heavy drops of a pending storm striking the canvas roof and the distant rumble of thunder.

"Think that's thunder or cannon?" Bobby Jenkins said.

"Thunder, "Joshua said. And then they heard the lonely whistle of a far off train. "Troop train. It'll be coming for us before too long. Harrisburg is kind of a rail-head for the northern trains and we'll be riding south on one of those to fight for the Union."

"I'm sure hoping that Sergeant Kelly is going with us to fight," Bobby Jenkins said."

"What makes you say that?" Joshua asked.

"Don't know," Bobby said. "I think he makes me feel safe."

"Sorta like your Pa?" Joshua said.

"Cain't say," Bobby said, "I ain't never had a Pa."

"You was lucky," Joshua said.

Bobby just sat down on a bunk and looked at Joshua.

The following four weeks were not fun but Joshua discovered he liked the daily regimen of drilling, learning military philosophy and battle tactics, followed by hours and hours of firearms and close-quarter combat training. Sergeant Dan Kelly remained in the forefront and assured the troops of Company A that he would be leading them into battle. Joshua soon began to look upon the gruff but fair sergeant with something close to hero warship. He reveled in the fact that Dan Kelly would be his first sergeant as they marched off into the unknown. Bobby Jenkins whined continually about army life but stuck with it and the day finally came when they were ordered to pack their gear and be ready for a train ride in the morning. Company A of the 98th Pennsylvania Volunteers was abuzz with excitement that night and sleep was evasive in every tent. Naive young men were eager to join in the fight against the Confederate Rebellion and mostly couldn't quit repeating all those rumors of glory in battle they'd been hearing for weeks.

CHAPTER FIVE

The March

"Yeah," Bobby Jenkins said, "they say the Rebs eat babies."

"Tain't true," Joshua said, "theys people just like us."

"Yeah well, they kill babies, then."

"Maybe," Joshua said. "But not on purpose."

The train ride south was uneventful but along the way the new volunteers were treated to areas of near total devastation. The United States was near its fourth year of the war with the Confederate States and the earth had been scorched throughout the south to include parts of Maryland and Pennsylvania. Burnt-out train stations became routine and farm houses and town buildings often lay in nothing but chard rubble. The train bridges they crossed over appeared to be built with fresh and raw timbers leading them to realize that that some bridges had been destroyed by the Rebs or maybe their own troops and had been recently rebuilt.

Eventually they began to see wagon-trains of Union ambulances staggering north with their beds filled with the dead and dying. Endless columns of war-weary and exhausted Union Troops were passed as they staggered north on foot along the rail-road rights-of-way. On the second day the sergeants and corporals pointed out the area of conflict for the first and second battles of Bull Run, or Manassas, as the south called it. They crossed the stream of Bull Run on a rebuilt trestle and were mostly distressed at the remaining battle debris and the muddy fields of deteriorating wooden crosses and sinking grave mounds that proliferated the countryside along the train's route. Not only a few of the new volunteers began to wonder what they had gotten themselves into and were already planning for some kind of clandestine escape homeward bound. A fearful unrest began to spread throughout the volunteers.

The far too enlightening train-ride was now behind Company A of the 98th Pennsylvania and the raw troops had experienced their first few nights bivouacked in the rain beneath dripping canvas tent roofs and on muddy ground, followed each morning with a breakfast of bacon, hardtack and coffee, then breaking camp and back on the road again for those who were sore-footed and bored. However, on this morning they had been informed that they were marching toward the 'fight'. Joshua witnessed a familiar sight from his past as he saw troops tossing away perfectly good equipment and clothes in order to lighten their loads. The yelling and threatening of officers failed to stem the flow into the ditches and bushes along the way. Trailing sutlers and profiteers cheerfully gathered the discards for their own use or to sell back to the suffering troops.

The road ahead was muddy and chopped up badly by the caissons and wagons that had gone ahead of the 98th Pennsylvania Regiment. The rain had slowed to a steady mist-like drizzle but a week of constant storm had left Colonel Pickins' regiment slogging slowing and wearily toward a imminent confrontation with Robert E. Lee and his Confederate Army of Northern Virginia.

"I heard them Rebs got some kind 'a scream when theys charge," Bobby Jenkins said. "I heard it's supposed to scare us heathen Yanks. But I ain't running from no Reb's screaming. Shoot'im between the eyes with a mini-ball, that's what I'll do."

"I see it all now," Joshua said, "General Bobby Lee Jenkins hiding in the bushes and peeing his pants while the Reb bullets are darkening the air."

"Will not," Bobby Jenkins said. "I'm gonna be a Union hero."

An officer on horseback road up and down the double line of marchers shouting at them to step it up and stay in formation. Joshua hated him. There he sat astride a horse all comfortable and without a drop of mud on his boots and uniform and yelling for the troops to 'step-it-up' and look sharp. The officer was cloaked snuggly in a poncho while most of the troops had tossed theirs aside on the first day of the march to lighten their loads. Joshua remembered months before when he'd watched with fascination as a Union regiments marched by the farm and witnessing many of the soldiers tossing away perfectly good ponchos and blankets, and had naively wondered why. Now he knew.

With some smugness he could feel the weight of his own poncho wrapped securely inside his bedroll shielded by a gum blanket. The march was Soberly hushed with only the murmur of the drizzle dripping off trees and brush alongside the wretched road, the occasional moans from bone-weary, home-sick troops, the snort of a horse, and the constant tinkle of mess gear strapped to the belts of the struggling men.

Slogging quietly next to the chatty Bobby Jenkins Joshua's thoughts returned to the farm and the warm memory of Katie Hespeth and her promise to wait for his return from the war. They had both agreed that there never would be anyone else for either of them. Now Joshua worried that she would grow bored with farm life and start seeing one or more of the local young men who frequented the Reverend Black's Wednesday evening prayer meetings and the Sunday sermons and church picnics that always followed in good weather. Then there were those monthly box-lunches where Katie always managed to mark her box so Joshua could readily out-bid all the others and share it with her. He longed for Katie now and reveled in those memories of when they had snuggled in the hayloft in her father's barn listening to the rain on the roof and making plans for when they would be married and live in town and Joshua would be a lawyer and she would teach in the little school house on the hill just on the edge of town.

Bobby Jenkins broke his reverie. "You think it was a good thing for Old Abe to take the Army of the Potomac away from General McClellan and give it to General Meade? Probably made Little Mac barmy."

"Huh?" Joshua said. "Oh yeah, I guess the president knows what he's do'in."

"But General McClellan consolidated all those armies and made kind 'a one big one," Bobby said. "Gosh General George Meade got kind' a lucky, there."

"Course General Meade is a jerk," Joshua said. "Least that's what the papers say. But I doubt it some. Prima Donna, that's what they called him."

Suddenly a low murmur emanated from the slogging troops. Some stopped in their tracks. Others collided with the back of the man in front of him, followed by curses. Soldiers started looking at each questioningly.

"Oh, oh," Bobby Jenkins said, "I heard it too."

"Thunder?" Joshua said. Shaking his head no.

"Ain't no thunder," the soldier behind Joshua said. "Thems cannon. And theys not our cannon. Gonna be hell to pay soon."

Then a rider galloped up to the front of the column and yelled something at Colonel Pickens. He was out of breath and looked anxious.

The marching column halted without orders and conversations erupted from all quarters. A minute later an officer rode by shouting.

"Colonel Smith's regiment has come under artillery fire less than a mile ahead. Prepare to skirmish. We gotta relieve him right soon. Quick-step. Quick-step now."

The officer rode on down the line. No one bothered to quick-step. The only sound was the distance rumble of cannon fire and the murmur of the regiment. Suddenly Sergeant Kelly appeared along the line speaking vigorously to the troops as he walked.

"You ain't veterans of battle yet, but ya'll gonna be soon. Thems veterans in Colonel Smith's regiment and they knows what to do under fire. We are gonna relieve them. Quick-step."

He walked on down the line repeating his words. Then two or three corporals appeared along the line, including Corporal Homan, shouting for the troops to quick-step. The entire line seemed reluctant to move, to follow orders. Corporal Homan stepped into the line next to Bobby Jenkins and kicked him in the butt. Jenkins jumped and grabbed the injury.

"Farm-boy, did ya'll here Sergeant Kelly. Quick-step it, now."

Then Corporal Homan kicked another man in the butt. The line began to move quicker but not anywhere near the so-called quick-step. Homan stepped back out of line and aimed his musket, waving it in the general direction of the column. "First sum-bitch that don't quick-step gonna git his ass shot off." He cocked the musket and aimed it at Bobby Jenkins.

Sergeant Kelly appeared trotting back down the line.

"Corporal put that musket down."

Corporal Homan frowned and lowered the gun, spun on his heels and stomped away without speaking to Kelly. Daniel Kelly turned to the troops, a slight smile on his lips, and spoke around his cigar.

"Now men, seems Jeb Stuart is trying his very best to destroy our wagons and supplies just up ahead and we gotta stop him. Colonel Smith's regiment is catching hell right now and I'll bet my ass he's hoping and praying were gonna run Jeb's cavalry and artillery off. So what you say we quick step and save Smithy and his regiment."

Silently the line of men turned and began to trot toward the rumble of cannon fire. Joshua Cole suddenly felt thirsty, his mouth filled with cotton. He wanted a drink and could hear the lovely sound of water sloshing in his canteen, but didn't venture a pause to uncork it and drink.

A half mile closer to the battle clouds of fluffy white smoke appeared on the horizon drifting peacefully away like mountain-sized cumulus. The rumble and roar of cannon grew stronger and the troops began to hear the rip of musket fire and the occasional scream of a wounded horse rising above the din. A quarter of a mile from the conflict Sergeant Kelly came trotting along the line yelling for the troops to form a skirmish line and to dump everything but weapons, ammunition, and canteen. Having been drilled day in and day out at Camp Curtin the troops quickly fell into a skirmish line. By now the road had widened and the forest had fallen back opening into meadow-like fields sprinkled with fading summer flowers.

If I survive this skirmish, Joshua thought, I'll be a battle veteran; a real honest to goodness soldier in General Meade's Army of the Potomac. I've got to write to Katie and tell her all about this. I'll send her kisses and hugs and the promise that

I'll be coming home after my enlistment is up and we'll get on with that life we promised each other. It'll be my turn to sit around Reverend Black's picnic area and tell glorious war stories.

Joshua's thoughts were suddenly interrupted by the sing-song of cannon balls bouncing along the road toward them and exploding cruelly among the first line of skirmishers... panicked men suddenly plunged into a hurricane of fire and smoke. Quickly a gaping hole of 10 or 15 men opened up in the lead skirmish-line as cannon balls exploded amongst them laying waste and leaving large gaps in the column. Sergeant Kelly could be heard over the commotion yelling at the troops to move forward and fill the gaps. Then men began crumpling to the ground as Jeb Stewart's sharp-shooters sighted on them. Some men lay writhing and moaning in the dirt while others curled fetus-like silent and motionless. Now the advancing Union troops were forced to leap over and around wounded men. Joshua leaped over a fallen soldier whose throat was spurting blood from a severed artery. A squirt sprayed Joshua's pant leg and brogans. He'd lost sight of Bobby Jenkins and felt another fear clogging his already pounding heart. Back at Camp Curtin he and Bobby had decided to stay close to each other when the shooting started, naively agreeing to watch each others backs. Innocent youths that they were.

Corporal Homan ran along the front of the skirmish line yelling incoherently, blood streaming down his face. Joshua ran forward and joined several others as they filled a new gap in the line. Joshua realized he was exposed to the next volley of cannon and musket fire and that lethal Rebel sharp-shooter precision. Within moments a man on each side of him crumpled into the dirt. Corporal Homan came running back to help fill the gap in the line but abruptly collapsed in a pile at Joshua's feet. Joshua was forced to step over him as the line now advanced into a sleet of bullets from a battle-line of butternut-clad Rebels down on their knees 50 yards ahead and firing rapidly at the Union advance.

An officer rode his horse into the skirmish line waving his sword and yelling for the troops to reform a line and advance. Before anyone could respond to his orders his horse bawled painfully and collapsed into the skirmish line scattering and tumbling troops. The officer rolled onto is feet shouting but was immediately struck by a bullet in the face sending his kepi flying and toppling him face down into the line of struggling men.

Then just behind the skirmish line the Union artillery, having moved into position, began firing over the heads of their own troops into the Rebels who had begun backing away from the cannon fire toward a dense tree-line fifty or a hundred yards behind them. In mere moments the Union artillery was quieted by the lethal accuracy of the Confederate sharp-shooters hidden in the trees as Union artillerymen fell wounded or dead beside their guns. Rebel cannon fire quickly commenced again and two Union guns were destroyed in explosions of debris and shattered bodies.

Over the din of cannon and musket fire Union officers could be heard yelling and ordering their troops to retreat. Sergeants and corporals quickly called for retreat formations wherein alternating riflemen took turns firing from the kneeled position, retreating, reloading, kneeling, firing, and retreating several paces again. Joshua Cole had speculated during training about what good could this often trained retreat formation be during battle. Now he knew. He silently thanked God that the officers had not called for an advance formation where he and the others would be carrying out the same drill but steadily moving toward the Rebs in that lethal hail storm of southern lead. Joshua winced at the plethora of bodies sprawled in the road as they retreated; some writhing in pain while others lie silent.

CHAPTER SIX

Battle Residue

They had bivouacked near a stream called Cat's Run. The conversations about the battle with General Stewart's Cavalry had faded in the two days since the retreat. The next morning a detail of 20 men under the supervision of Sergeant Kelly had been sent back to the site of the previous day's battle to gather the wounded, the dead, and any equipment that might have been abandoned. Joshua Cole and Bobby Jenkins were amongst the 'volunteers'. Actually Sergeant Kelly had walked through the line of tents pointing at individuals and yelling, "You, you, and you, are volunteering to return with me to the battlefield."

Joshua Cole dreaded returning to the site. As they'd hastily retreated from the Rebel onslaught he'd been very aware that bodies were left on the field and road and that even some of the wounded had been calling for help. He even remembered how one of the artillerymen had been entangled amongst the wreckage of his cannon, his insides protruding out through a massive gash in his stomach, and laying there crying out for help and calling for his mother. Josh remembered the sight of the artilleryman's boots and had the thought, "had he known when he pulled those boots on this morning that it would be his last time?'

Flies buzzed noisily at the battle site as Sergeant Kelly, grim mouthed, directed Joshua Cole, Bobby Jenkins and several others to form a burial detail while the remaining troops gathered up weapons, gear, and ammunition left on the field and road. In a halcyon field of dying summer flowers Joshua and the others dug a fifteen foot long trench two feet wide and three feet deep. Eight bodies lay piled at the edge of the trench. Sergeant Kelly and a corporal examined the dead trying desperately to find something identifying on each body so a record could be made of those lost and buried. Joshua recognized the dead artilleryman, now bloated, blow flies laying their gruesome eggs on his drying bowls creating a home for their maggot children who would in time sprout wings and begin their search for another lifeless body to feed on, breed, and generate their dreadful progeny. He recoiled at the scene of this hideous slaughter pen…created by the tender of man's blood offerings.

Joshua cringed at the touch of these swollen, grisly, and smelly bodies. These human beings that had just a day ago been alive with hopes and dreams for a life not lived. The dead artilleryman appeared to be no more than 20 years old. Joshua had the feeling that he wanted to know his name and to go home after the war and tell his kinfolk why he had died and how. He wanted to tell them where to find his grave so that they could visit him and leave flowers and maybe make a gravestone to honor their son, husband, lover, or father. Joshua couldn't help but remember something he'd read in a book about life by some renown 18th Century author. The author had written something about life and death. He'd wrote that 'it was not that you had died that counted, but how you'd lived and why'.

The dead were laid on their backs, head to toe, with pieces of woolen blankets covering their faces. Sergeant Kelly ordered a separate group of men to shovel the dirt and rocks back into the hole. The corporal had taken a piece of a shattered ammunition box and created a marker with the those names that were obtainable, the date of death and burial, and the regiment number, and placed it in the ground at the head of the trench. Then Sergeant Kelly, in his gruff manner, cigar stub in a corner of his mouth, said a few words over the dead. The remaining corpses of Confederate soldiers were buried in a separate trench from the Union men. When Kelly spoke he directed his comments toward the Rebels as well as his own. Joshua Cole's nascent respect for Dan Kelly swelled.

"Oh Lord, take these here fallen men into your arms and bless them with your love. They have fallen as heroes of this here Union Army and while fighting for what they believed and trying their damn best to put down a rebellion against these here United States. Ashes to ashes, dust to dust. These fallen men are now gathered to their fathers. Amen."

Joshua saw it laying there in the dirt, in the bloodied dirt, the black-blood dirt, and then a breeze picked it up and blew it against his foot. It looked like a letter, grayish paper, wrinkled, frayed, bloodied. Joshua picked it up and stood reading the contents, it was a letter home, not mailed. A letter that would remain not mailed. He opened the single page and fingered what appeared to be a bullet hole through the paper with a crimson ring of blood about the hole. He stood there amidst the battle wreckage and read the letter.

My very dearest Margaret and sons,

They are saying that we will be moving out in a couple days but maybe as soon as tomorrow. Therefore I may not write to you again for some time. I feel that I need to write you once more because this may be my last words. That glorious Union Army of Grant's is closing in on us and we're gonna fight to the last to save our homeland and our glorious south. The colonel has passed down the line that the next few days may be a challenging-one of battle and death to many-maybe me. If I fall on the field of battle it is God's will and I give my life willingly for my country and my people. Should I fall I beg you to go on joyously with your own life and I know you will forget me in time and that is only natural. Grief is destructive to the soul and spirit. You have always been the strong one. Be there for our boys as you have always been.

My thoughts on this night while I lay down to rest with more than 2000 other soldiers are too many of these lads are enjoying their last night on earth. But they will go to their rewards with Jesus. I know. But most are only boys. Some of them remind me of our sons. The strength of my love for you and the children is bottomless on this night that is likely my last. My friends here are pinning notes on the backs of their coats with their names and family so they will not be buried unknown. Some folks say that the dead revisit their loved ones and if this is true I will come often in the night. When I am gone I will send you feathers as a sign of my love for you and to show you I haven't forgotten you. As you go through your life and see a feather floating near you or on the ground it is that love message from me."

Love you all, Daddy

Joshua folded the letter carefully and put it in his coat. It was well-written; probably by a Confederate officer. He would decide later what to do about it. Would he mail it or write his own letter to the family. He walked away hating all this death and destruction and couldn't help but think back to those bygone days when he had listened avidly to those stories told by returning army veterans and innocently believing all those *rumors of glory.*

The smell of the dead still lingered in the air, on the hands of the soldiers, and on their clothes. Joshua remembered the smell of days-old dead animals and couldn't help but think that dead humans reeked the same way. It was a smell that lingered in Joshua's nostrils all the way back to the bivouac and kept him from eating his hard tack, salt pork and coffee that evening.

The sun disappeared behind a ridge and a half moon appeared, lighting the white 'A' tents and brightening the glow of camp fires and somehow quieting conversations stemming from around the camp. In a hospital tent at the edge of camp Joshua could hear the moans of the wounded, like the moaning of an ill wind. He knew that the body of Corporal Homan lay wrapped in blood-soaked blankets in a tent and couldn't help but feel sadness and compassion for 'General Farm-boy.' The army surgeons had done all they could for the wounded. The morning after the battle Joshua had watched while a detail of three men carried severed arms and legs to a spot behind the tents, dig a hole, and without ceremony or heed, bury the amputations. Joshua wondered if Katie Hespeth would still love him if he came home without a leg or arm, or even eyes. One of the dead had been shot directly in the face, but mercy had taken him away within hours after the battle.

Joshua tried, without success, to quell a desire to visit Homan. He cringed at the thought of seeing this hard-nosed corporal mangled for life, that is if he survived at all. But he walked reluctantly toward the hospital tent, something driving him on. Did he really desire to see Corporal Homan impotent, the meanness drained away, or did he care enough to want to do something for Homan? The odor was there, even outside the tent. Joshua drew back the flap and peered into the gloom. A candle flickered in a tin lantern atop a wooden hard tack box. Homan's face glistened with sweat. He was awake and staring straight up into the gloom. The heat in the tent was stifling. Joshua inched forward to the edge of Homan's cot. For a long moment Homan didn't move and then slowly turned his face toward Joshua, the eyes mere holes like cigarette burns in a wool blanket.

"What you do'in here Farm-boy," he croaked in an near muted voice, attempting to rise up. Joshua put his hand on Homan's shoulder and gently let him back down. Homan moaned and gasped for air.

"Sir, I came to see you, Sir," Joshua whispered.

"Why'nt ya'll wanna do that, Farm-boy?"

"Because you're my corporal, sir."

"You ain't too bright, Farm-boy."

"Bright enough to know that my corporal is hurt and that I wanna check on him."

"Well, while you're here could you git me a sip of that there water over there? And…that's not an order."

Joshua got the canteen and poured some into Homan's open mouth. Water dribbled out and ran down his glistening cheeks.

"Taste like it was poured out'a someone's boot," Homan mumbled. "But thank you, Private Farm-boy."

"Any thing else I can do, before I leave?" Joshua asked.

"You can write me a letter to my lady."

"I can do that, "Joshua said.

"Right now you git," Homan said, "Because I gotta sleep some."

Joshua reached out and took Homan's hand. "We'll do that letter in the morning, first thing, Corporal Homan."

"Much obliged, Joshua Cole." Joshua smiled. That had been the first time Homan had referred to him by his full name.

"I'll see you first thing in the morning," Joshua said.

Joshua reached and took Homan's hand. It was hot. Fever, Joshua thought, this man is burning up. Before closing the tent flap Joshua looked back and saw that Homan was still staring straight up into the gloom.

Pink dawn. The sun rising over an eastern ridgeline. Cook fire smoke drifting up and then flattening out on the hushed morning air. Men speaking quietly, drinking coffee and eating fried salt pork and hard tack biscuits, some smoking their first pipe of the day. Joshua approached the company clerk and begged a quill, bottle of ink, and paper. He went to the pot bubbling over the fire in front of his tent and poured his tin cup full of coffee, said good morning to Bobbie Jenkins, and then walked to the hospital tent with Corporal Homan. Homan looked worse than he had the evening before. He had quit sweating and his skin looked as dry, inert, and as shrunken as the mud left exposed in a late summer riverbed.

Joshua was repulsed by the stench emanating from Homan and the cot of a man next to him. Homan was silent and unmoving. There were no lighted candles. The mauve glow through the canvas roof from the morning sunlight illuminated Homan's face. He turned slightly and spoke haltingly to Joshua, his voice cracking and without moisture.

"Farm-boy, what ya'll do'in here?"

"Good morning Corporal Homan. The letter. Did you forget? You wanted me to write a letter to your wife. I've coffee."

"I cain't drink no more," Homan said, "my throats sort 'a closed off."

Joshua lit the candle and placed the paper on top of the hard tack box and looked at Homan. "What would you like me to say?"

Homan was silent for a long moment. "Lillian. Lilly's her name. She be my wife now for more 'in two years. We gotta baby girl, MaryAnn."

Joshua began to write as Homan labored to speak.

Dearest Lillian and MaryAnn,

Hope this here letter finds you well. I really miss you and the baby. I heard there was a fever go 'in about Pennsylvania and I'm hoping to the Lord you ain't got it or MaryAnn. We went to war with some Rebs two days past and I got hit pretty hard but don't worry none at all. Maybe they'll send me home soon and we can be together again. They've got good army doctors here and they are helping me all the time. A private named Joshua is helping me write this here letter. He is an okay private and a real good soldier in a fight. He looks after me some. I'll be home soon and don't worry none about me.

Love you both too much,
Daddy Jim.

Joshua made sure the letter to Lillian Homan was in the army satchel and ready to go out with the next detail. Then he walked back to Homan's tent to tell him the letter was on its way. As he approached the tent the flap opened and a surgeon came out wearing an apron with day-old blackened blood stains.

Joshua saluted. The captain did not salute back. "Can I help you? private?"

"I...sir...I came to tell Corporal Homan that his letter is on its way home."

The captain shook his head. "He's dead."

"Sir?"

The captain shook his head, turned and walked away.

"He's dead God damn it," the captain yelled.

Joshua wrote another letter to Lillian Homan later that day. He sat by the evening fire drinking coffee. He didn't feel much like eating. Bobby Jenkins sat on a log across from him eating salt pork and hard tack mixed and stirred with other found ingredients that was something the troops had begun calling Coosh. The sun had set in the west but a warm light still shown on the mountain ridge to the east.

"So old General Farm-boy is dead," Bobby said. "Well, good riddance, I say."

Joshua looked up from his writing shook his head and scowled.

"Private Jenkins."

"Well, he was meaner than cat shit."

"Weren't not," Joshua said. "Before he passed he told me he was trying his hardest to teach us civilians something about this here army and about fighting. Trying to give us some discipline that might get us through this here war without being kilt or worse. He was a veteran of that terrible battle at Gettysburg…you know?"

Bobby Jenkins poured the remains of his coffee on the fire.

"Well he got himself kilt, didn't he? He weren't no smarter than no one else."

Joshua ignored Bobby Jenkins and finished his letter to Corporal Homan's wife.

Dear Lillian Homan,

My name is Private Joshua Cole. Me and your husband are friends. It is my sad duty to tell you that Corporal Homan passed to the Lord this day in the morning. I was with him to near the last and a company doctor was with him at the last. Corporal Homan was a good man and a very good soldier. It won't help you much but he was a real hero in that fight that kilt him. He didn't whine much about his wounds and he spoke about you and little MaryAnn all the time. He sure loved you very much. Too much he said before he passed to the Lord. Maybe someday if I git through this here war I'll come and see you. God bless you and the baby. And, I'll try to send his stuff.

Private Joshua Cole
98th Pennsylvania Volunteers
Army of the Potomac
Cat's Run, Virginia

Ps I will see that Corporal Homan gets a proper burial and marker so you and the girl can visit him some day.

CHAPTER SEVEN

Double-Quick

"Sergeant Kelly wants to see you right now, double quick," Bobby Jenkins said, as Joshua entered the tent the morning after Corporal Homan died.

"He just left, madder' in hell."

"What'd he want?" Joshua asked.

"Shit, I don't know but he looked mean."

Joshua stopped at Sergeant Kelly's tent flap. "Sir, Private Cole reporting as ordered."

"Don't stand out there in the heat Cole, git in here."

Sergeant Kelly was sitting on his bunk writing. He was smoking a cigar and was stripped down to his graying cotton uniform shirt and trousers. His walrus-like mustache was askew and drooping some over his mouth. His boots had been lying just outside drying in the heat. His bayonet was hanging from a tent pole and his musket was standing in a corner. The cigar smoke smelled pleasant and Joshua thought he might like to try one sometime.

Kelly continued to write.

"Sir?" Joshua said.

"I'm bringing this log up to date Cole, all because of you."

"Sir?"

Corporal Homan recommended, before he passed, knowing he was gonna die soon, God rest his soul, that you, of all God damned people, take his place. Well, man proposes and God disposes."

"Sir?"

"That's right. And I'll be damned if I know why. Hell Cole ya'll still green, even though you are a battle veteran now. And, you did good in that skirmish with the Johnnies. But, the captain and the colonel both seem to agree, so well, God damn it all, sew some corporal strips on your sleeve and start do'in your job...today! Report to me in a couple hours and I'll try my most to git you started. Besides, were moving out today so there is one hell of a lot of work to do.... You git more pay, you know?"

Sergeant Kelly stood up, a slight grin sneaking out from behind the cigar and mustache. He shook hands with Joshua and then handed him a cigar. "Learn to smoke these damned things, they'll make you look a bit older...God damned pup. Now git go 'in Corporal Cole."

"Sir, I don't have any stripes," Joshua said.

"Hell Corporal," Kelly said, "I didn't take you to raise. See the Quartermaster."

Joshua found the quartermaster and obtained a set of the double stripes then dug through his haversack to find his 'house-wife'...or rather, his sewing kit. It took three struggling tries before he was satisfied with the way the stripes fit his sleeves. Putting the sack coat back on made him self-conscious and dreadfully reluctant to step out of the tent. When he did the much dreaded howls and cat-calls erupted from the troops nearby. He walked away as quickly as he could.

'A' tents were stowed in the wagons and the caisson ammunition wagons hitched and ready to roll. The remaining cannons lined up to the rear of the column with their packets of black powder safely stowed beneath thick wooden boards.

Several hundred bored troops were ready to move out and seek a new adventure. Bivouac was comfortable the first two or three days but then a pandemic restlessness began to spread throughout the camp like a slow virus working its way from man to man that could, and often did, cause problems. Fist fights were a common problem with the troops when personal space became too personal. Fighting amongst the troops was ever-more dangerous considering the ready availability of lethal weapons. Officers and sergeants had to be constantly on the alert for trouble and take immediate steps to quell problems even if it required severe punishment, court-martial or even death. The company colonel was not above shooting a violent trooper.

Sergeant Kelly was leaning against a caisson with an unlit cigar in his mouth. Joshua Cole was standing to near attention in front of him, new corporal stripes sewed haphazardly onto his sleeves. He felt self-conscious with his new authority and had an over-whelming urge to cover up the stripes with his hands. It was even worse when he heard a few snickers emanating from the troops standing nearby.

"Ya'll don't gotta stand at attention Corporal Cole," Kelly said. "Now listen up. Ya'll's job as corporal is to help me keep these here troops in line and I don't want you to show favorites or be a piss-ant that's afraid to chew ass. And remember the good job Corporal Homan did rousting you…Farm Boy?"

Joshua grinned remembering his first army designation. "Yes," Joshua said, "…sir."

"Now listen up some more," Kelly said, "you help me inspect the troops when it's necessary and you take charge when I'm not around. I want ya'll to act like a sergeant. Help git the troops moving on the march and help get them situated when we're trying to set up our bivouac. Can ya do that Corporal Cole?"

"Yes sir," Joshua said. "I can sure learn how to do all that."

"Well I'm hoping you're a fastlearner because were in one hell of a war here and we ain't got time to piss around. So don't be sitting on your ass when there's work to be done. Earn your pay."

Sergeant Kelly moved safely away from the caisson and stopped to light his cigar. Then he turned back to Joshua and made a casual salute. Joshua returned it and then smiled to himself, and then he looked down at his new stripes and nodded toward them. He had decided days before that he would follow Sergeant Kelly to Hell and back if he asked it.

CHAPTER EIGHT

The Railroad Riot

"We're gonna march toward Remington double-quick. Headquarters has ordered this here regiment to stop the looting, killing, burning and raping that's being done by our very own troops. Seems they've gone wild after drinking wagon loads of apple brandy and after hearing that some of our own troops has been out-rightly murdered by some local folks. Fact is I heard that one of our troops was kilt by having a stake driven through his eyes. Anyhow, we all gotta march up to Remington and try to calm that regiment down a might. You gotta remember though, these here Pennsylvania fellas are our own brothers and we ain't gonna hurt none of these if it can be prevented. Now ya'll gonna have to grab a root and growl."

Joshua and the rest of the regiment stood at parade rest while the captain rode his horse back and forth in front of them delivering his instructions. Word had come down that a Pennsylvania regiment had gone berserk while destroying a rail-head in the Confederate back-woods town of Remington. Some of the Union troops had started burning private homes after looting them and in some cases raping the women and killing the men who were unfortunate enough to be home. Rumor was that a Union colonel had actually raped a young pregnant woman in front of her children. Banks and stores had been looted and the post office burned.

The regiment formed up quickly and began the march toward Remington at double-quick leaving their artillerymen and supply wagons behind. Each trooper was ordered to carry an extra 30 rounds of ammunition and enough rations for 3 days; their haversacks smelling of lead and gunpowder. The march was compounded when the captain realized they were on the wrong road and were forced to retrace their steps four or five miles and start over again. There was considerable soldier-like bitching and complaining down the line as tired and foot-weary troops resented the idea that soldiers from their own army needed to be reprimanded and restrained. Mob behavior had become all too common during this angry war when rage and hate became overriding following the vicious atrocities committed by both the north and the south.

A soldier in line was heard to yell out, "Fuck'em Reb folks. Let our boys have'im. Yeah! Let them have'im for supper. Theys ast for it."

A lieutenant rode back from the middle of the column toward the noise, pulled his horse up and demanded to know who was doing the yelling. No one spoke and all eyes were turned away from the lieutenant. Ignored, he turned and rode back toward the front of the column.

"I won't be hear' in it again," he shouted back over his shoulder.

Chuckles and snickers emanated throughout the line of soldiers.

Two minutes later the same offensive voice was heard again.

"Fuck'em Rebs. I ain't 'bout to fight my own brothers for no gawd-damned Rebs and not for no boy Lieutenant nor no boy captain. That's what I say. Yeah! How 'bout you donkeys? What ya'll think?"

No one answered. There was silence in the line, the only sound the tinkle of tied-on mess-tins, the creak of leather and wagon wheels and the muffled sounds of brogans and boots scuffing the dirt road.

A first sergeant walking beside the column had spotted the cheeky soldier. He stepped into the line pulled the man aside and confronted him. The column halted as if by order, the troops continuing to stare straight ahead, not wanting to be addressed by the big sergeant. Every last trooper in that regiment knew that you didn't dispute anything with First Sergeant Daniel Kelly if you wanted to remain upright and unmarked by a verbal dressing down or even the occasional gloved slap to the side of the head. Officers had been observed paling slightly in verbal confrontations with the big Irishman.

"What was that you said 'bout our officers?" he said.

The trooper and the sergeant stood staring at each other. The soldier broke and looked away. He attempted to walk away but the big sergeant grabbed his arm, nearly jerking him off his feet.

"I asked you a question, "Sergeant Kelly said.

The trooper dared a look back at Kelly, then looked down at the big fist gripping his arm and made a weak attempt at shaking it off.

"I said top-o-the morning to ya'll Sergeant Kelly," he mumbled.

Then a crack was heard throughout the column and the soldier sprawled backwards into the dirt, his mouth and nose spurting blood. Sergeant Kelly loomed over him. The soldier reached for his bayonet scabbard. Kelly put his foot on the outstretched arm and shook his head.

"You think you can keep that big mouth of yours shut?" Kelly said.

The bloodied soldier pulled his arm from under Kelly's boot, rolled over and staggered to his feet and swiftly took his place in the column. He wiped his nose and mouth on his coat sleeve and began to walk ahead, giving the soldier ahead of him a slight nudge. There was silence in the line.

Kelly looked around at the others and nodded and then resumed his walk beside the silently moving column while lighting a fresh a cigar.

Bobby Jenkins moved ahead hastily with one eye aimed at Sergeant Kelly, hoping he wouldn't be called for it. He took a position just behind Joshua. His move didn't go unnoticed by Kelly.

"Corporal Cole," he yelled, "Suppose you can start earning your pay by help 'in keep these troops in line?"

"Yes sir, Sergeant Kelly," Joshua said without looking at him.

"I helped put those there stripes on your sleeve and I can sure as hell rip them off," Kelly said.

Joshua chanced a look at Sergeant Kelly. Kelly was grinning.

Bobby Jenkins snickered.

"I'm gonna rip those stripes off your sleeve Corporal Cole if ya'll don't start earning your keep," he whispered.

"Shut up Bobby," Joshua said.

"Quiet in the line," Sergeant Kelly yelled.

Joshua dared a glance at Bobby Jenkins. Jenkins snickered again.

"Corporal Cole. Ya'll gonna be promoted to private. Ya'll a piss-poor corporal anyway."

"Shut up, Bobby."

"Well I ain't gonna shoot no yanks," Bobby said.

The sun had set and twilight was looming over the landscape.

Sergeant Kelly had announced that they were within a couple miles of Remington. He'd added that "when we git there ya'll gonna have to grab a root and growl, 'cause it ain't gonna be easy."

Sergeant Daniel Kelly walked silently, listening all the while to the familiar sounds of marching troops. His mind was far away in the Indian Wars of the late fifties. He was chasing Geronimo and his band of Apache outlaws in the Arizona Territory. Geronimo's wife and children had been murdered and he was on the warpath. Geronimo had become a true leader of the Apache Nation but was never actually a chief. Kelly had been a corporal of cavalry in those days before the rumblings of a civil war surfaced. But now in his reminiscing he was back astride his assigned horse, Smoky Joe. It was hot in the Arizona desert. The day before he had killed his first human being and later, after the skirmish was over, he'd examined the remains. This little Apache warrior hadn't been more than sixteen years old when he died quickly from Kelly's heavy bullet with most of the back of his head shot away. Once again Kelly felt the grief he'd known that night lying awake in his blankets and looking up at the same stars that that Indian boy had probably looked at on his last night. His first sergeant had ordered him to "scalp the little bastard." Kelly remembered resting his hand threateningly on his carbine and watching the rough sergeant grin and then walk away shaking his head.

Breaking his trance he thought again, and probably for the thousandth time in recent years 'To hell with this crazy world,' and then suddenly yelled, "Shit," while some of the marching troops dared venture a glance his way, warily remaining silent, not nearly bold enough to question the sergeant's peculiar outburst. But they all knew that Kelly could do unusual things and was never to be questioned; even the officers wisely refused to question Kelly. Dan Kelly was 'old army' and most officers were either volunteers or created via political appointment. West Point graduates often found themselves promoted to higher rank and found themselves commanding brigades, divisions, or corps.

A low ridge stood dark and foreboding between the marching troops and Remington. Above the ridge a layer of low clouds seemed to glow in an Heaven-like radiance. The glow became ominous and threatening and the men soon began whispering amongst themselves. A fear of their own troops began spreading through the line like an unrestrained illness.

"I think that there hill is called Preacher's Ridge...I think," Bobby Jenkins said.

"That's right, "Joshua said. "But what's that glow in the sky?"

"A warning from God," a soldier mumbled. "Shit, we're off to fight our own troops. God's gonna frown on us tonight."

"Yeah," another said," but God's on our side."

"What makes you thinks so?" another said.

"God is always on the side of right."

"Which side is that in this here war?"

"Ain't right, them southern folks slaving niggers the way they do."

"Ya'll think God loves niggers?"

"Don't call them niggers, theys folks like anyone else. Theys love their children and each other same as us."

"Fact is," another said, "I heard most of the darkees die on those slave ships on the way over here from Europe."

"Ain't Europe you idiot, it's Africa."

"Book I read about it says they chain them black folks up in the hold of the ship and just let them die off. No food, no water, no nothing."

"No...white folks wouldn't do that," a young soldier offered.

"Bull shit Jackie. I heard them black folks just lay there chained for weeks in they own shit and vomit. I even heard that the sailors some times go below and rape those black girls and women."

"Why not? Another said.

"Cause it ain't right, you ass, that's why."

"In that book I read it says when the darkees die the sailors just throw them overboard for the fishes to eat."

"Yeah, but I heard the English Navy captures and hangs them slavers and scuttles their ships."

"God bless those Englishmen," another said.

"I heard that the English Navy is the greatest in the world."

"Yeah, and they been thinking real hard about siding up with the Johnnies."

"Ain't no business of the English to do that, whats I say."

"I think it's damn admirable of them, scuttling them slavers like that."

Another, just to Joshua's left spoke up. "That Pennsylvania regiment must be burning a hundred houses and buildings. Guess that's what's lighting up the sky."

"I hope not," Joshua said.

"Quiet in the line," Sergeant Kelly roared. "And, they ain't burning no hundred houses. Ain't no more 'in 35 or 40 buildings in that whole town."

An hour later as Joshua's regiment approached the town it was clear that Remington was burning. The captain halted the column and gave his final instructions before they marched into town and into the middle of a drunken, out of control, brutal clash. The Pennsylvania regiment had gone wild, the officers losing any semblance of control. Officers repeatedly threatened to shoot rioting troops but declined as their own lives were threatened by drunken soldiers. Local store houses had been looted and casks of apple brandy had been broken into and shared amongst the troops. Some casks had been opened by firing a bullet into the barrel, then filling tin cups and canteens from the spouting brandy and then setting the highly flammable liquor afire.

Troopers could be seen staggering in the flame-lit streets with their tin cups sloshing over with brandy and shooting wildly into buildings and houses. Flames scorched the night sky above the tiny railroad village as soldiers gathered embers from one fire and tossed them into unlit houses and buildings. Civilians had been shot without cause. Dead bodies could be seen laying on boardwalks or in the doorways of burning buildings. Men and women had been murdered for merely protesting the violence. The owner of a mercantile had been tied to a cracker barrel in his storeroom and the building torched. His screams were heard by others in the street but armed, drunken soldiers had prevented his rescue, threatening death for anyone who tried. This Pennsylvania regiment was no longer and army, it had become a rioting gang of drunken criminals.

"Arrest that man," the regimental captain order Sergeant Kelly.

Dan Kelly spun around toward the captain. Captain Jacobs was sitting astride his horse in the glow from the burning buildings, his saber drawn and resting vertically against his right shoulder.

"Sir?" Kelly said.

"Arrest that colonel...now," Jacobs ordered.

Dan Kelly lifted his musket and pointed it in the general direction of the horseless Union colonel.

"Ya'll under arrest sir by order of Captain Jacobs," he said.

The Union colonel's hand went to the butt of his revolver as he said, "I'll have you both hung for this."

Kelly cocked his rifle as the colonel began to draw his revolver...Kelly took careful aim at the colonel's chest, shaking his head.

"Very careful sir," he warned. "I'm under orders."

Captain Jacobs' second in command, a first lieutenant, rode up and saluted.

"You sent for me captain?"

"Take custody of this here colonel and then find a place for a stockade for these drunken fools, including this here colonel. Shoot him if ya'll have to. Set a heavy armed guard on the stockade. Now git."

The lieutenant looked down at Kelly with his rifle still aimed at the colonel.

"The colonel, sir?"

"Yes lieutenant," Captain Jacobs growled, "this gawd damned colonel and his gawd damned drunken troops."

"Sergeant Kelly," the lieutenant said, "disarm the colonel."

Kelly took the colonel's pistol and sword and handed them up to the lieutenant. The lieutenant drew back as if he was afraid to touch them.

The colonel was staring up at Captain Jacobs and the lieutenant.

"Captain, I repeat, I'll have all three of you hung for this."

"Colonel sir," Jacobs said, "I'm under direct and written orders from General George Meade himself to quell this here riot and to arrest the negligent officers, and ya'll is number one. More to follow. You will have company when you are hung."

"I won't be hung and you'll pay for this, Captain," the colonel said. "I'm a West Pointer and so is General Meade. Georgie and I go way back. You'll regret this. Meade would not have me arrested if he was here. Trust me, I'll have your ass for this."

"That's to be seen, Colonel," Jacobs said. Then he wheeled his horse and rode away leaving the young lieutenant and Dan Kelly to deal with the colonel.

By the time the sun was coming up over the eastern hills the fires had receded down to ghost-like smoking embers. The railroad village of Remington no longer existed. The once bustling main street was now a desolate alley of burnt black timber remnants and smoldering piles of ash. The morning air reeked of drifting ash and smoke. Joshua's regiment had been able to return order to the formerly rampaging troops with minimal force. A Union soldier had been shot to death during a three man skirmish and several regimental officers had been arrested and corralled along with the rest of their troops. Near one end of the smoldering town a livery stable had survived the holocaust and now held more than a hundred Union troops sitting sick and dejected and guarded by soldiers with muskets and fixed bayonets. Many suffered wounds from their foray into Remington and the conflict with the town's citizens and Captain Jacobs infantrymen.

By mid-afternoon the former rioters had vomited, sobered some, drunk coffee and attempted to eat salt pork and hard tack and had been formed back into a semi-orderly regiment. A burial detail had been selected from amongst the culpable and the decimated town and surroundings explored for the bodies of the dead and the down. The bodies of 3 Union soldiers had been found killed by the townspeople, and it was true, a Union soldier had been discovered with a wooden stake driven through his eye. The Union colonel and several of his subordinates were destined for a confrontation with the commanding officer and a court martial. The remains of the dejected regiment and it's officers were marched back and assimilated into new companies attached to General George Meade's Army. Later exploration of the town disclosed that the train rails had been torn up, heated and bent into uselessness. The town bank had been robbed of everything of value. Captain Jacobs later commented during the court martial that the Colonel's troops had accomplished some things during their misbehavior; tearing up Robert E. Lee's railroad supply line and cleaning out a southern bank of it gold and silver and confederate money. It was testified to that destruction of the railroad and the confiscation of any monies, gold and silver was the original intent of the attack on Remington. The colonel was relieved of his command, reduced in rank to major, and sent back to Washington and placed in an administrative roll signing miscellaneous documents and aiding the Quartermaster's office in ordering food and weaponry and helping keep the railroad supply lines open and running. He resigned his commission at the end of the first month. Captain Jacobs and Sergeant Dan Kelly never saw him again after the court martial.

CHAPTER NINE

Battle at Cedar Ridge

They marched, well walked, because there really wasn't much evenness in the way they moved. Their boots, the wheels of the caissons, and the clip-clop of the horses made a musical rattle-thump as the column picked its way along the wood-plank road. In some places the planks, or logs, were rotted all the way through and the horses hooves would fall into the abyss stopping all progress from that point back until the unfortunate animal could be freed by much yelling and cursing. The real worry was that a horse would break its leg when it dropped through. A horse with a broken leg had to be shot. And worse still, the plank road was not level in most places due to weather and heavy use and the caisson drivers and horse artillerymen struggled to keep their equipment from sliding off the planks into the swampy mires on each side of the road. It had been raining off and on, but mostly on, for 3 days.

In the week since they'd pulled out from Cat's Run Joshua Cole had begun to understand the duties of a corporal and felt for sure he was satisfying Sergeant Kelly at least some of the time and was discovering that he enjoyed possessing a modicum of authority. He was beginning to feel like a genuine soldier of the Army of the Potomac.

Joshua Cole was walking along the edge of the plank road and occasionally summoning the courage to yell at a straggling troop to 'step-it-up'. His orders were frequently met by cat-calls and scorn. A few of the older troops frequently referred to him as 'boy'. Joshua didn't allow the disrespect to distract him from his duty and he was learning to dress down those that enjoyed mocking him. Gradually the troops began to accept him as a leader and from time to time he was even addressed as 'sir'. Sergeant Daniel Kelly kept a close watch on Joshua's behavior and even on an occasion or two threatened to rip the stripes off his sleeve if he didn't start acting like a corporal. That bit of encouragement usually boosted Joshua Cole's self-respect and forced him to openly confront the troops with renewed energy and force, especially when Sergeant Kelly was within ear-shot.

Rumor was that they were going to attack a Confederate entrenchment at a place called Cedar Ridge. The officers had spent considerable time extolling the virtues of trenches which the Union Army had been reluctant to utilize, while the Rebs had discovered that it was much safer to shoot from a hole in the ground rather than a well-formed, close-gapped skirmish line. The Rebs had also begun building barricades of fallen trees and stones when-ever they intended to stay put awhile or contemplated confronting Union troops at any given locale. This would help protect their supply route to the north and enable them to continue to provision Robert E. Lee's Army of Northern Virginia. Lee wanted desperately to re-cross the Potomac River and move on Washington while pushing its way deeper into Pennsylvania and maybe even Maryland. But Lee hadn't forgotten the beating his army had taken at Gettysburg in July 1863. They'd told that Maryland was still a neutral state but they were 'damned' sure that there were some Rebel contingents that had been fashioned there by southern sympathizers and profiteers. Lee's failure at Gettysburg had begun to demoralize the Confederate Army and a renewed threat toward Washington and Abe Lincoln might restore hope to the besieged Confederacy.

The intelligence produced by cavalry disclosed that the Reb Army was spread out along Cedar Ridge and even formed fish-hook formations at each end of the ridge to keep the main body from being flanked while protecting gun batteries positioned on the crest. Word was from the officers that attacking Cedar Ridge would literally be an up-hill battle, meaning troops would have to climb the ridge, or God-forbid, charge up the slope exposing themselves to enfilading fire without much coverage while fighting the heat and resulting up-hill exhaustion. The fear of canister shot from the cannons spread throughout the ranks. They all knew well that canister, dozens or even hundreds of lead balls in each cannon charge, would and could devastate a charging skirmish line of troops, and especially if they were charging uphill into the scorching flames of gaping cannon muzzles. Officer had assured the troops that Union Artillery would set up a half-mile or so from Cedar Ridge and bomb-bard the hillside and crest for several hours before any infantry attack would be mounted. What they had strove to omit was the fact that the Rebel artillery on the ridge would be blasting the Union guns from the high-ground, a definite advantage. At Camp Curtin, during training, the officers had regularly taught that, if you must fight, fight from the high ground.

They camped a mile or so from Cedar Ridge. The entire army was able to screen itself in a copse of trees and brush that covered a hundred acres or more. The hope was that Reb cavalry would not spot them in the meantime. The order was sent out forbidding campfires, leaving the troops to congeal in the cold night air after eating raw salt pork and hard-tack biscuits. Considerable grumbling drifted throughout the camp as soldiers exhausted from the 20 odd miles march that day had been looking forward to hot coffee and food. Pickets were stationed and the rest of the troops erected 'A' tents, ate cold food, then sat in front of their tents, where a fire would have been, smoking their pipes and cigars.

Just before dark sergeants and lieutenants came through giving orders for the troops to clean their weapons, fill their canteens, store one days rations in their haversacks, collect 60 rounds of ammunition, and be ready to move on Cedar Ridge at daybreak. The Union cannon bombardment of Cedar Ridge and the Confederate camp were to start before dawn. Speculation around the camp by troops was that the early cannon fire would signal a following infantry attack allowing the Confederates to prepare for the battle. Others voiced their opinions that they didn't want to charge up that ridge without preceding cannon fire. The common word around camp was, "Blow then Rebs all to hell before we have to go up there," and, "Maybe we won't have to."

The entire camp grew grimly silent as one might say, 'the calm before the storm'.

Joshua Cole was ordered to continue making rounds of his regiment encouraging the men to follow orders and be ready to fight at dawn. As he moved throughout the tents he became aware of the change in mood from the days march. The men were mostly hushed, staring off into nowhere or quietly conversing, writing letters, or trying to nap. On his stroll through the regiment he became aware of a new phenomenon, at least to him. Men were writing their names on pieces of paper and pining them to the backs of their sack coats. Joshua was reluctant to ask the men why, so he walked to Dan Kelly's tent.

"Sergeant Kelly, Sir," Joshua said as he stopped in front of the tent.

"Come in Corporal. If you must."

Joshua pulled back the tent flap and saw Kelly laying on his back, arms behind his head, a cigar glowing in his mouth. He was in shirt sleeves and trousers with his suspenders down and partly hanging off the bunk. There were holes in his wool socks. He turned and looked at Joshua.

"Sit."

Joshua sat on the empty bunk across from Sergeant Kelly.

"Cigar?"

"Yes Sir Sergeant Kelly, that would be appreciated."

"On the box. Light it with the candle."

"Prefer to save it for later Sergeant Kelly."

"Up to you. What ya'll want?"

"Well sir, the men, some of the men, are writing their names on scraps of paper and pining them to the back of their sack coats."

Kelly turned and looked at Joshua. "And?"

"Well sir I'm not at all sure why they'd be doing that."

"Jesus Corporal Cole, you are green. Aren't ya?"

"Yes sir, I guess I am. I think I read something about it but I ain't sure."

Kelly suddenly sat up and swung his legs around toward Joshua. He sat there for a long moment staring at the ground between his feet, then he looked up at Joshua, reached over and put his hand on Joshua's shoulder.

"Because a lot of them, probably more than I want 'a think about, are gonna die tomorrow. Maybe you and I. They want someone to know their names when they are found dead out there on that hillside. They want someone to mark the grave and maybe let the kinfolks know what all happened to them so kinfolk can come visit the grave when this here war is over."

Joshua put the cigar in his mouth and lit it with the candle. He sat looking at Sergeant Kelly. Kelly was nodding.

"You gonna do that, Sergeant Kelly?"

"Ain't got no kinfolk so it don't matter. No one to care that much."

Joshua got up and walked to the tent flap, stopped for a moment and then looked back. Kelly had lain back on the cot.

"It matters to me Sergeant Kelly."

Kelly took the cigar out of his mouth and looked at Joshua for a long moment then smiled. "Yeah? Well now git the hell out' a here Corporal Cole and care for your troops...and...I ain't your father."

"Yes sir, Sergeant Kelly." Joshua saluted and stepped out of the tent.

"You don't need to salute me," Kelly said. "I'm no officer, either"

Joshua turned and looked back at the tent flap. "Yes sir."

Kelly spoke again. "Good luck tomorrow Corporal Cole. You'll need it."

Joshua sat alone in his tent, smoking the remains of Kelly's cigar. He was thinking about what Kelly had said about the name tags. He wondered if he should make one and pin it to the back of his sack coat. If he did would that create a bad omen? An omen that would for sure send a bullet his way? He decided not to tempt fate. Instead he thought he should write letters, one to his mother and one to Katie Hespeth. He borrowed ink, paper and quill and began to write. *My Dearest Kathleen, It has been close to a coon's age that I've written to you. We been on the march every minute and tenting every night. I'm a corporal now and have to prod my troops to git stuff done on time. My sergeant, Dan Kelly, keeps a close watch on me and won't let me shirk my duty. But Sergeant Kelly is a good soldier and I think he is my friend. He gave me a cigar to smoke tonight. I kind of like cigars. We are going to fight the Rebs tomorrow on a place called Cedar Ridge. Some of the boys are writing their names on pieces of paper and pining them to the backs of their coats so if they're kilt someone will know who they are and where they're buried. I didn't make one. My corporal was kilt in the first battle but didn't pass for two days so now I'm the corporal. His leaving for God's Pastures was pretty awful, he suffered some and I cared for him a little before he passed. We buried him alone and not in a mass grave like the others. It has been raining mostly for three days and everything is wet. The cannon folks are real worried their black powder is wet. Theys gonna strike Cedar Ridge before dawn before we charge them Rebs entrenched up there high. They've got holes to shoot from and big piles of logs and rocks. We call those things redoubts. We are praying the cannons will finish the job before we gotta climb that ridge without no cover much. Well dearest Katie it's time for me to turn in and git some rest for tomorrow. Don't you worry none. God is watching over me. God and Sergeant Kelly, that is. Your servant, Corporal Joshua Cole, Company A, 98*[th] *Pennsylvania Volunteers Army of the Potomac Oh yes, say hello to Missus Hespeth.*

Joshua dropped the quill pen sat up straight and listened. He dropped the remains of the cigar in the dirt, got up and opened the tent flap. The sun was nearly down with enough remaining light to perceive troops on their feet around the camp and all looking about and shaking their heads. Something wasn't right. Then it happened. The Rebel yell, or scream, as it was. Then chaos and confusion. Gunfire rattled the twilight, men screamed and fell to the ground, clutching wounds or silent. Joshua was aware of a pit, pit, pit noise and then realized the tedious sound was bullets punching holes in his tent. Butternut clad figures were dashing through the Union bivouac firing pistols and rifles and hacking at the startled soldiers with bayonets and rifle butts. Stacks of Union muskets were kicked to the ground by Rebs as Union soldiers attempted to arm themselves and fight back. Joshua saw unarmed Union soldiers running, scattering, and fleeing into nearby trees. He yelled, ordering Union troops to turn and fight, but his plea fell on deaf ears. He felt that he was yelling soundlessly into a rampant wind. Men were screaming as they fell face down into their own blood offerings to this vicious sneak attack by the Confederate Army. It had been dawdling for the Union officers to think that the Rebel cavalry would not quickly discover the Union camp.

Joshua turned into his tent and reached for his musket and bayonet just as his head suddenly numbed, leaving nothing but ringing in his ears and in the obscurity of his blackened vision lost his balance falling to his knees, the gun tumbling away. He fumbled for the edge of his cot and tried to get back up as darkness descended on him leaving him oddly aware of his face in the dirt and sand on his lips and wetness running into and behind his ears. The back of his neck felt wet. His last fretful thought was that he must get up and fight and that Kelly would think him a shirker.

It seemed an hour, or a day, or a month later that he found himself attempting to spit dirt out of his mouth. He was vaguely aware that his face was against the ground and that his cheek was in a pool of wetness. As his head cleared he became aware that the wetness at his face was vomit. Clearing his eyes he raised up slightly and could just make out the puddle beneath his head. There seemed to be streaks of crimson mixed into what was left of his stomach contents. The odor nauseated him further. Reluctantly he let his face and head fall back into the ooze from his own body. He tried to sleep. He wanted very much to sleep. To let the pain and nausea fade into nothingness; into oblivion. At this moment he desired oblivion more than anything he had ever wanted. The oblivion would not come; oblivion is not always kind, he thought; beautiful oblivion, alluring sleep, why it would not come to his rescue and set him free?

Sounds came to him from outside his tent. He attempted to discern them in the darkening recesses of his mind. Were they cries? Was a baby crying? Was it Katie Hespeth crying for him? A voice called for its mother. Another voice cried out "Holy Mother of God help me." Another voice called out "where's the doctor?" Then he thought he could smell smoke. Camp fire smoke? No! The smell was canvas burning. The tents were burning. His tent was burning. He could feel the growing heat on his deficient body. He needed to get up. He ordered his legs to move but they were heavy and tingling. He tried to get his face up out of the ooze but failed. It entered his mind that the only thing to do now was to sleep, and sleep, and sleep. His last conscious thought before total obscurity was that someone was pulling on his legs. He had the sensation of being dragged along the ground. He felt fear! Where they burying him? He tried to scream, "I am not dead," but nothing came out. Were they going to put him in a hole with other of those dead? Those stiff and paling corpses. Would they throw dirt into his open eyes? Would they crush him with rocks? Would they say those same meaningless words over his grave? Would they save his personal belongings and send them to his mother? Would they mark his grave? No, they wouldn't, he knew that. He would be in the same hole with a dozen other rotting corpses and no one would ever know where his final resting place was, if you could call that horrifying fissure a resting place. Katie Hespeth would never know where he lay; would never know what had happened to him. Something he had heard in church began to run through his mind, "into the valley of death…the valley of death…the valley of death. Then all faded and he entered that dark place of nothingness, of future nothingness, of total and lasting loss.

CHAPTER TEN

Prisoners

It was morning, or maybe evening. The sun peaked through dark clouds and what there was of it caused Joshua's eyes to pain sharply. He blinked and wanted to close them again and go back to sleep. A dull ache permeated his head. He reached up and felt something wrapped around his skull. A rag. The rag was tacky and the spot he touched caused him to jerk his hand away. He forced his eyes back open and the scene before him began to focus and then clear. The devastation repulsed him.

The Union camp, or what was left of it, was fraught with ruin. There were no tents standing. Fifty feet in front of him was a pile of muskets and odds and ends of other recognizable Union equipment and gear. Almost directly in front of him was a pile of logs, neatly stacked. Logs? A closer scrutiny showed that it wasn't logs at all, but dead Union soldiers, their feet bared with nothing but filthy and well holed socks to protect them from the morning chill. Fifteen, twenty, maybe more, lay dead still, their war over. Then it hit Joshua. Rebel troops were famous, or infamous, for taking the boots or shoes off dead Union troops. Joshua had heard that all too often Confederate soldiers marched in their bare feet, their brogans worn to nothing and with not a hope-in-hell of replacements showing up. After all, he thought, wasn't it the search for shoes that actually got the Gettysburg fight started? Slowly he became aware of other Union troops sitting on the ground close by. Some were wounded with rags wrapped on various head or body wounds. All were silent. Some laying on the ground, others sitting and staring blankly into some vacant and mysterious void. Directly behind this small group several Confederate soldiers stood guard with fixed bayonets, apparently hoping that a Union soldier would make a run for it. Make a run for it? Then Joshua noticed that his own brogans were gone.

A tall dark man in butternut gray approached the group of prisoners. He wore a luxuriant full black beard and smoked a thick cigar. Joshua saw the colonel's insignia on his coat. He walked up in front of the group. Some of the Union soldiers tried to stand and some even attempted painful salutes. The colonel smiled and raised his gloved hands, shaking his head.

"Sit! You don't have to salute me. I'm the enemy. You are my prisoners and I'm hear to tell you what's gonna happen. After we talk to you for a time and you bury your own dead, I'm gonna line ya'll up and shoot every damned one of you Yanks. So now the longer you talk to us and give us the intelligence we need the longer you'll live. Maybe even live long enough to have a last meal. A meal that is of salt pork and hard tack. Just maybe a cup of coffee, seeing as we have your supply now. Maybe a last meal is in order, but maybe not. But we'll likely not waste it on you. It'll just dribble out through those holes in your Yankee guts after we shoot you. Too wasteful."

Joshua struggled to his feet, his head throbbing, nearly overcome with dizziness. "You can't shoot these here men. We're prisoners of war and you gotta treat us fair and square. The Union Army don't shoot your folks when we capture them."

The colonel shook his head, "You do, and we will. Corporal, what's your name?"

"Joshua Cole, sir."

The colonel looked away toward the morning sky and then back at Joshua. "You ain't related to the Coles of Pennsylvania are ya?"

"Yes sir. Thems probably my folks and grand-daddy and grandma."

The colonel shook his head, walked over and shook hands with Joshua.

"I know your folks. My daddy done business in Pennsylvania with you Yankee farmers. Poor merchandise though."

Joshua didn't speak but backed away and sat down against a tree.

The colonel turned and started to walk away, then stopped and turned back. "I ain't gonna shoot any of you Yanks, someone else might, but I won't." Then he walked away and was lost in the mix of troops and chaos.

A Confederate sergeant appeared in moments. He was big, deep chested, bearded, dirty, ragged, and his left leg was bandaged above the knee with bloodstained rags. He stood facing the men with his bandaged leg slightly raised off the ground, while leaning on a crutch made from a tree branch. In a strange way he reminded Joshua of Sergeant Dan Kelly.

"I'm Sergeant Hawthorne and ya'll gonna git up now and go over there and bury your own dead. Theys shovels over there and you're gonna dig a trench right next to them dead Yanks. Bury them with no fanfare and no preacher. If you wanna say words or gather stuff for theys folks ya'll can do that. You yanks is body robbers anyway. Let's get started."

Joshua and the others, those that could walk, moved slowly to the pile of stiffening corpses. Flies buzzed even though the day was young and cool. Joshua felt that he could smell death on the air. The smell reminded him of dead animals in the woods or the rotting remains of deer he had gutted. He looked at his own remaining troops and saw no officers, sergeants or corporals, so he realized it was his duty to take charge of the surviving Union soldiers.

"You men there grab those shovels and dig a trench alongside these men of ours and we'll bury them as proper as we can."

"Corporal," one of the Union soldiers spoke up, "We gotta identify these here dead fellas for theys families."

"I know that," Joshua said, "I'll go through their pockets and such. Some of them got papers pinned on their backs with their names."

Joshua approached the dead soldiers. In his mind he called it a stack, and then immediately cautioned himself, "There is no such thing as a stack or pile of dead human beings," he said aloud. "Especially my soldiers."

"What?" one of the Confederate guards yelled?

"Nothing," Joshua said.

"Well git go 'in and bury them fellas before they start to stink worse then they already did."

Joshua turned and walked over to the mouthy Confederate soldier. His head was spinning, the dizziness trying to take over. He knew he was wobbling.

"You Rebel boys seem to have no respect for the dead. Put that musket down and tell your boys to stay off and we'll sort out this rotten mouth of yours."

"Sounds good to me," the soldier said, grinning and looking at the other guards.

"Put the gun down" Joshua said, feeling his head throbbing and a vague nausea invading his stomach. He was sure he had a fever. His skin was dry even though his clothing was damp and clammy. In his heart he knew he would lose any fight with this Confederate soldier but felt he had to stand up for right and especially in front of the Union troops he was now responsible for. Then relief happened.

Sergeant Hawthorne suddenly appeared. "Drop it," he yelled. "Ya'll git to work. Now."

Joshua turned and walked to the gathering of dead Union soldiers and began rolling the dead onto their backs. He felt ashamed because he didn't really want to touch the dead. His hands seemed to numb as they came in contact with the stiffening corpses. It seemed as though the Rebs had stacked the bodies all face down, as though no one wanted to have to look into those lifeless eyes. After he'd gently rolled a couple of the dead off the pile he cringed, staring at the next prone body. Sucking in his breath he wanted to turn away but knew beyond a doubt who the dead soldiers was. Then he reached down and took hold of a stiff arm and gently rolled the corpse over and onto the ground. Bobby Jenkins' sightless eyes stared back at him. Bobby's chest was soaked with drying blood and his face was as white an early snow in Pennsylvania. Joshua backed off and sat down in the dirt, fighting back tears. An hour passed before a private approached Joshua.

"Corporal," a young soldier said, "we need to move on with this here burial. Can you manage? I know that Private Jenkins was your best friend in this here army. Sorry." Then he reached and put his hand on Joshua's shoulder.

Joshua looked up from his place at the edge of the trench. 14 dead Union Soldiers lay stacked head to toe and one on top of the other in the narrow ditch. Bobby Jenkins' body was on the top of one of the stacks. Joshua had wrapped him carefully in rags he'd manage to find. Looking down at the body of his friend he could hear Bobby say, "Corporal Cole, I'm gonna rip those stripes of your sleeve if ya'll don't start do'in your job. Ya'll a piss poor corporal anyway…sir." Joshua smiled, came to attention and saluted.

"At ease Private Jenkins, you don't have to call me sir," Joshua said, fighting back tears. "Good bye friend. If I live through this I'll for sure see your ma."

The other dead suffered dirt onto their faces and bodies but there was no alternative. The Confederates were not about to provide blankets to cover the dead. Joshua had removed Bobby's personal belongings in order to return them to his family. Sergeant Hawthorne had said he regretted not being able to provide blankets nor coffins for the dead Union soldiers.

"Yes private," Joshua said in response to a plea from a young Union soldier.

"You ain't gonna let these Rebs shoot us are ya?"

"Not if I can help it, but I reckon I don't have much to say about it."

The private shrugged. "My daddy is a preacher and I can say some words I learnt from him over these dead fellas if you want?"

"That would be nice, "Joshua said. "Let's bury them and then you can say those words."

With the mass grave filled in the young soldier took a place at the edge of the abyss, cleared his throat and said the Lord's Prayer from memory.

"Our Father, who art in heaven,
hallowed be they name.
The Kingdom come,
They will be done,
On earth as it is in heaven
Give us this day our daily bread

And forgive us our trespasses,
as we forgive those who trespass against us.
And lead us not into temptation,
but deliver us from evil.
For thine is the kingdom, the power and
the glory. For ever and ever. Amen"

He followed with,

"Lord, please bless and take these here fallen soldiers unto your arms. They died fighting for justice and they deserve eternal peace in your loving care. Ashes to ashes, dust to dust."

Sergeant Hawthorne approached as the graveside words were being said. He waited, hat in hand, leaning on the tree branch, his face in pain.

"You gonna march south with the rest of this here regiment and take a luxurious train ride to a place in Georgia we call Andersonville Hotel," he said. "The train ride will take a day or two. Don't be expecting anything special. Ya'll the enemy and ya been kill 'in my folks for about 3 years now, so we ain't got a lot love nor sympathy for any Yankee dog."

One of the guards spoke, grinning. "But ya gonna love our luxury hotel, 'specially built for you Yankee criminals. Lots of sunshine and a little rain and lot's a leisure time to think about how ya'll Yanks are try 'in to kill us Southern folks off. Save them niggers. Yeah, that's it."

"That's enough," Sergeant Hawthorne said.

Joshua was sitting on the ground amidst the other Union prisoners. He'd heard of that notorious confederate prisoner of war camp called Andersonville. The rumor was that prisoners were bivouacked in the open without as much as a tent over their heads, practically nothing to eat, and with a creek running through the camp as the only source of water...and, he'd heard that the creek served as a latrine. Typhus, diarrhea, and starvation were taking a dozen or more lives every day and that there was a killing field in the woods nearby where they buried the dead in open pit trenches without as much as a holy word over them or any kind of a marker to let the world know who or how many was buried there.

Joshua's company commander had talked to the regiment about these Andersonville Prison rumors and had said that when the war is over and the Union has prevailed every guard and their commanders at that prison were going be summarily hung without benefit of trial or for sure even a modicum of mercy. And he said that a firing squad would be too good for those Confederate scum and that seeing them dangling and squirming at the end of a rope would be joyful and very satisfying and the only justice they deserved. And he'd reaffirmed that God was on the side of the Union and that every Reb would eventually burn in hell for his sins, and he said that he'd heard that some Rebel general called 'Stonewall' Jackson had preached that God was on the side of the oppressed south and that the Union camp would live in hell for all eternity as its final reward for the suppression and genocide of the southern nation and its people. And that, he said, was pure blasphemy spouted regularly by those southern heathen. 'Stonehead' Jackson, that's what he is. Devil's advocate as such."

The following morning, after the prisoners had suffered the 'forbidding clouds of night,' Joshua and the other Union prisoners awoke to a misty rain and wet wool blankets. They sat shivering beneath trees that dripped icy globules of fluid onto their heads and necks and trying to eat petrified hardtack biscuit whilst avoiding, as best they could, the wiggling little maggots that crawled and squirmed as they were picked out of the dough and tossed aside.

"Hot coffee would be more than welcome," a private said to no one in particular. "Hell, even tea. Hell, even hot water."

Another private tossed the remains of his breakfast into the bushes.

"This is nothing but Rebel pig shit."

Joshua turned. "Enough Private. Eat it. You're gonna need your strength."

"Ain't not," he said, "I'm going out of here right now."

"You ain't, "Joshua said. "Hold tight."

With that the private jumped to his feet and made a run for the nearby trees. A crescendo of shots rattled the air like ripping cloth and the private crumpled into the bushes and lay still. Joshua got up, looked at the trio of Rebel shooters and walked slowly to the body. A bullet had entered the back of his head and exited through his face, taking most of it away and a plethora of brightening red splotches appearing on his back. In a way Joshua envied the dead private. It was over for him. His fighting and suffering was finished. Hopefully in this lasting final peace he was home with his loved ones.

Sergeant Hawthorne appeared and ordered Joshua to bury the dead man.

CHAPTER ELEVEN

Andersonville

It was a cattle car with manure and damp straw inches thick on the floor. There were no blankets for warmth and no buckets of water to quench raging thirst and no predictable latrine other than a chosen corner of the cattle car. Suffering prisoners were frequenting that corner with what had become known as 'the Tennessee Two Step', diarrhea. When needed men squatted in that corner while the others tried to busy themselves by staring through the cracks in the side of the car. Their only elation was the thought that a Rebel soldier was stationed on top of the car, shrouded in a rain slicker, and probably suffering nearly as much as they. Joshua and the other Union soldiers sat huddled together for warmth. No one spoke and the only sound was the click-clack of the train wheels representing a message from some evil specter reminding them that their hunger and death was eminent. Through the wall boards they could see rain and the sky black and ominous without light. The train was pulling them south toward Andersonville, Georgia and a date with an unknown but nearly predictable destiny. Joshua sat in a corner with his back to the slated sides of the cattle car. Droplets of rain dripped through wetting his coat and slipping down the back of his neck. His head injury wept constantly, still covered by the filthy rag the Rebs had wrapped around him the night of his wounding. A dull ache remained behind his eyes and at times his vision seemed to blur and only the severe shaking of his head could cause them to clear. He sat thinking about the past few days, weeks, and months. He was saddened that he had failed to keep those personal items he'd retrieved from Bobby Jenkins and Corporal Homan. He'd wanted to be able to return those items to their families after the war was over, and tell them how they had died in battle and that they died as heroes and good soldiers. But would he survive. He thought about the rumors he'd heard about that notorious Rebel prison at Andersonville, Georgia. Rumor was that men were dying every day from starvation, disease, and exposure. Some said there was a short log barricade just a few feet inside the main barricade and if a prisoner even touched it he was immediately shot by the guards, even eagerly. Some said that suicidal prisoners would touch the barricade or try to jump it just so they would be shot in order to escape that hell-hole, the only possible way out. Word was that no one had ever escaped and those that tried died from the rifle accuracy of the guards or immediate summary execution. He'd heard that some of the prisoners became outlaw raiders and preyed on their own weak and helpless, stealing their clothes and any meager food supplies they might have. Word was that the raiders even killed their own kind. A form of human desperation had consumed most.

Joshua's trance was broken by the sound of weeping. The source was a young soldier near his own age. The soldier was leaning back against the wall, his face in his hands. Joshua crawled over and sat next to him. The soldier looked up, tears streaking the grime on his face. Joshua put his arm around the soldier and sat quietly staring off into the gloom of the cattle car.

"I'm hungry and want to go home," the soldier said.

"We all do," Joshua said quietly, "and we will." The others were watching.

"And I hurt so bad."

Joshua looked at the soldier. "Where you hurt, Private?"

The private reached down and pulled up the trousers of his right leg. Joshua drew back at the sudden stench. There was a long black gash running from the ankle to just below the knee. It was caked in blackened coagulated blood with streaks of green gangrenes puss oozing from the bottom of the wound and running into what was left of the wool sock.

"Bayonet?" Joshua asked.

"No sir, saber from one of those Rebel Cavalry bastards. Did it after I'd already been captured. Did it just to be mean."

"You hang on. Soon as we git to Andersonville we'll git a doctor to clean it up and put on a proper bandage."

The private just looked at Joshua with obvious doubt in his eyes.

"Will they cut my leg off? I can't go home without my leg."

Joshua knew he was lying about the doctor and about any care the the private might get at Andersonville.

"Not likely! What's your name?"

"Davy…David…Brooks."

"Where you from, Davy?"

"Maryland. My daddy's a pig farmer up there. My momma's gone to be with the lord when my baby sister was birthed. I joined up to fight the Rebs but…"

"What town? Or what area?"

"Brookside…, Brookside, Maryland. But we live out a bit."

"What's your daddy's name?"

"Same as me, David. Some folks call him Big Dave 'cause of his size and strength. I took after my momma. I ain't too big, but I'm farm strong."

"I bet you are."

Joshua was memorizing all the information the private could give him about his family and homeland knowing that it was very unlikely that Private David Brooks would survive the gangrenes illness in his leg. He'd learned that gangrene invasion into a leg wound soon traveled to the opposite leg and then to the heart killing the victim slowly and painfully. Joshua reached up and placed his hand on Davy Brooks' forehead. He felt fever and aridity. The infection was already affecting the entire body.

Joshua knew that if he himself survived the war, he would need to write to David Brooks and tell him how and where his son had died.

Davy Brooks spent the night whimpering, groaning and tossing about. Twice he was heard calling out for his dead mother. Then as the day lightened up Joshua found him cold and stiff, his eyes open and staring sightless into the gloom. With help he moved Davy's body to a far side of the cattle car and covered his remains with straw. No one spoke, the only sound the monotonous click clack of the train wheels as they ground slowly on, in the rain, toward Andersonville Prison.

The following morning as the sun was coming up the train slowed and then stopped. Voices were heard and then someone unchained the cattle car door and Confederate soldiers aimed muskets into the gloom and ordered everyone out. Joshua took one last look at Davy Brook's straw covered body and moved toward the door. A Rebel soldier grabbed Joshua by the trouser leg and yanked him out of the cattle car tumbling him onto a train rail. Joshua rolled over and kicked the soldier with his right foot, the soldier cursed as he fell between the tracks, his musket clattering near Joshua's right hand. He reached for it.

"Keep your hands off me you sum-bitch," Joshua screamed, kicking again at the fallen man, while trying to seize the fallen musket. A second soldier ran to Joshua, kicked the gun away, and struck him in the back with the butt of his musket. The first soldier regaining his feet kicked at Joshua, striking him in the face. Joshua heard his head ring and then go numb, hot wetness spurted from his head wound, mouth and nose and then a slow dark shadow crossed his vision. Somewhere in the night that covered him he was with Katie Hespeth again and they were walking through a meadow in knee-deep wildflowers infused with acres of golden and orange poppies. Katie was holding his hand and leaning against him with wisps of her hair tickling his cheeks. He could smell her usual rose fragrance and see the red of her lips; that same red that her mother objected too calling it cheap and often threatened punishment it didn't stop. Then the illusive image shifted from the meadow and Katie was holding his head. The coolness of her hands on his fore-head and face was pleasurable. He felt at peace, but his back hurt. Then abruptly he saw a grave in the meadow. It frightened him. Was it his grave? The grave was fresh dug and the earth covering it was sinking in. A rough hand-fashioned cross was tilting over and near the head of the grave a bouquet of flowers had wilted and collapsed. Now he was lying in bed but the bed was strange with rock hard lumps that hurt his body and the blankets felt hot and sticky. He wanted to tell Katie about it but his voice would not come. He wanted to reach and touch her but his hands and arms would not work. He could still feel the tickling wisps of her hair against his cheeks. Slowly his vision began to clear, causing a glaring sun to burn his eyes, so he closed them and tried to go back to Katie Hespeth. She wouldn't come back and had gradually withdrawn those wonderfully cool and silken hands. Her rose scent was gone, now replaced by an offensive odor he could not identify. He struggled to turn his head away but couldn't move. Suddenly Katie reappeared but now her lips had paled. Her face sobered as she drew back from him, unsmiling, gradually fading into smoky wisps of fog and then vanishing.

"Kate…Katie…what's wrong. Why'd you leave?…Come back Katie…please come back."

A man's voice came through, rough and deep. Then Joshua smelt him. It was the odor of a filthy, unwashed human being."

"Corporal I ain't Katie, but I am First Sergeant George Hall, Company A, Second Massachusetts Volunteer Cavalry. Wake up damn it."

"Who?" Joshua managed to mumble.

"Sergeant Hall."

"What?"

"Wake up for God's sake and git on your feet."

"Where?"

"Andersonville…Reb prison. Wake up."

Joshua's head began to clear.

"What time?"

"By the sun…'bout noon."

"I'm hungry…starved."

"Well Corporal, we'll order you a steak."

"Water?"

"In the creek. We all call it Stockade Creek. Ya'll gotta stick your face in it while try 'in to avoid the turds."

His vision fogged, cleared, fogged again, and then cleared. The man on his knees next to him was heavily bearded and wearing what was left of a gold trimmed Union sack coat bearing faded first sergeant stripes and some sort of non-military trousers. His hair hung to his shoulders and was matted and filthy. Joshua thought he could see bugs crawling in the beard, the front teeth looked rotted and broken. He blinked them away.

As his head and vision cleared Joshua remembered getting kicked in the face and a fearful reality began to settle in. He was in Andersonville Prison and this first sergeant hovering over him was a prisoner and by appearances, a long time prisoner. Joshua tried to remember what little he knew about Company A, of the Second Massachusetts Volunteer Cavalry; vaguely recalling something about them being mostly California boys.

"Kin ya set up, Corporal?"

Joshua struggled to a sitting position and for the first time looked around and surveyed his new home. He didn't like what he saw.

He was surrounded and being stared at. Two or three dozen men were silently gawking at him. What Joshua saw froze his blood. These apparitions had once been men. Forms once tall and straight, these formerly stalwart individuals were now walking, staring, staggering, pitiful, skeletons. They were filthy, long hair and beards were matted and looked as if they could be filled with vermin of every kind. What remnants of clothing they wore were in rags and dark with grime and grease. Joshua could smell them. He could smell the animal filth of long time unwashed human bodies and layers of encrusted dirt. His gaze moved away from the men and surveyed the prison grounds. Piles of fresh and petrified human excrement dotted the enclosure. Near the center was an area that resembled a swamp supporting reeds in marsh-like stagnant pools of water. Shabby stick and grass constructed lean-tos dotted the grounds and were seen to be occupied by many more of these Andersonville Prison specters, some reclining on rags or bare dirt and some laying unmoving, lifeless shells of humanity.

"Sergeant, where's my troops?"

"Don't concern yourself with them boys," Sergeant Hall said, "theys mostly dead."

"No. Can't be," Joshua said.

"Seems your boys, what there was of them that still could, raised a little hell after ya'll was kicked in the face and seems theys done some harm to them Reb boys. So's this Reb Colonel, bless his sumbitch heart, had them lined up in front of the train and shot. Sumbitch made us all watch agin the threat of death itself. Cain't be two, three of your boys left. You was spared 'cause you snore 'in like a train whistle and a corporal. Corporals and sergeants and such are trade 'in stuff when it comes to exchanges. You know, exchanging troops for troops. Of course I ain't been lucky enough."

"Where are they?"

"Chained…chained right after the Colonel had them bury theys own dead, including that stinker ya'll hid under the straw."

"Davy Brooks," Joshua said.

"Yes sire," Hall said, "your Private Brooks was get 'in to stink right bad. Theys no trouble find 'in him."

"Can ya'll help me see my troops?"

"Well corporal I ain't gonna tote ya. Git up."

Joshua struggled unsteadily to his feet. The rocks and gravel dug into what was left of his wool socks. His knees wobbled and he started to fall but was caught by Sergeant Hall. It was then that Joshua noticed how bone thin Hall was and how the hand on his arm quivered.

"That's a right nasty wound you got on your forehead," Hall said.

"Joshua reached up and touched the wound. "Reb mini-ball."

"You ain't real pretty either with all those lumps and bruises on your face," Hall said. "Them Reb boys worked ya over pretty damned good before your boys got to them. Yes sir, it was one hell of a good fight. Your boys accounted for themselves quite well. You would 'a been proud."

"I am proud," Joshua said, "but they went an got themselves kilt on my account. I wouldn't have wanted that."

Both of Joshua's men were chained to what was left of a tree in the center of the compound. Dried blood caked their faces and blue welts half closed their eyes, and below, split lips shrouded what Joshua could make out as jagged and broken front teeth. He stood, supported by Hall, and stared unbelieving at what remained of the two men.

Both men were sitting in the dirt, their legs manacled to a large chain encircling the tree snag. They had been stripped of their trousers and sat bare-assed in the dirt. They looked like two captured, pathetic creatures.

"Took their pants," Hall said. "The Rebs do that to humiliate them in front of the others. Bastards everyone of them."

"Corporal Cole, fancy meet' in you here," one of the men offered.

"Welcome to Hell," the other said.

"You boys shouldn't have done it," Joshua said.

"We all didn't like one little bit what them guards did to ya'll."

CHAPTER TWELVE

The Hanging

They were marched to the dead remains of a large tree located near the center of the compound. Their hands were tied behind their backs. Their feet were bare and bloodied. The clothes that remained were ragged and filthy.

Their hair and beards matted and snarled. Their unseeing eyes were sunken deep into the sockets. They staggered. One fell and was kicked and dragged back to his feet, kicked again. He resumed the march toward the dead tree. A long protruding limb supported two ropes tied with 13 ring hang-man's nooses swinging slightly in the breeze. Those prisoners who could still walk had been forced at gunpoint to encircle the tree. A column of Confederate soldiers stood at attention, their rifles shouldered with fixed bayonets glinting in the early morning sun. A colonel stood at the front of the regiment, his sword out of its scabbard and held upright on his right shoulder. The four Confederate soldiers herding the two condemned men were silent. Joshua was now familiar with the *'Dead Line'*. The Dead Line was the barricade a few feet inside the stockade walls where if a prisoner had the audacity to approach it or even touch it, he was instantly shot to death by eager guards with itchy trigger fingers. Trigger fingers that wanted to return home after the war and tell the grandchildren how many yanks it had shot down during the War Between the States. It stood there, ambivalent toward the menace it imbued. The 'Death Fence' had actually became the 'Suicide Fence' for those overwrought prisoners who wanted to escape any way they could. It was a quick and painful death versus a slow and agonizing one. Often a prisoner would choose the painful way out.

The Sun was pink and just rising over the eastern hills, or more so, the eastern wall of the stockade. The two were standing on ammunition boxes: Confederate, marked 500 54 caliber, Richmond Arsenal. Their heads were shrouded with black hoods and wetness could be seen darkening below where the eyes were. They were sobbing openly and the crotch of one was wet. They were booth shaking visibly. "God bless Abraham Lincoln one of them yelled." Then on the colonel's command, a dropping of his sword, the boxes were kicked away leaving both men dangling, their feet kicking, while strangling slowly, their necks unbroken in a way that would have, in a vile scheme, been quick and some-what humane. After several minutes they quit struggling and hung silent and still, the only sound the wind high up in a cloudless sky. Then the colonel walked over to the dangling men, drew is revolver and shot them. He turned and spoke to Joshua and the others.

"Cain't be too sure," he said, grinning. Then ceremoniously blew the smoke away from the end of the revolver barrel. "Let this be a lesson to you Yanks. The heathens of the Union States think they know what's best for the country, but that ain't so. My fathers and grandfathers have farmed this here land for centuries using the backs of black folks and that's a tradition that shouldn't and will not be broken. God bless Robert E. Lee and God bless Jeff Davis."

"Here, here," was heard from the standing troops.

"God bless Abraham Lincoln," a voice was heard from the assembly of prisoners. The colonel turned and stared into the crowd. "I hear that again and someone else is gonna die today. And not by hanging." He raised his revolver over his head and fired one shot.

Joshua stood there his begrimed and whiskered face contorted with rage. Silently he vowed to spend the rest of his days killing Rebels and particularly that Confederate Colonel who had orchestrated the execution of his men and this entire demeaning display of hatred towards these two Union soldiers and…the entire cadre of prisoners.

"I'll see you hang for this," Joshua shouted, raising his fist. The other Union prisoners joined in a similar chorus.

"Watch your tongue, Corporal," the Colonel said. "Watch your tongue very close." He waved the revolver in Joshua's direction.

"Corporal what's-your-name," the big sergeant yelled at Joshua, "bury your dead." Then he ordered half a dozen armed soldiers to accompany the burial party. Joshua turned to the man next to him and nodded. The ragged soldier nodded back and the two of them walked to where a pile of shovels and picks-axes lay. In the two weeks Joshua had been in Andersonville he had been assigned burial duty almost on a daily bases. On some days a half dozen or more emaciated Union soldiers died from starvation, malaria, or at times by their own hands or the hands of others, to include trigger-happy Rebel guards who were all too pleased to improve their aim by sniping at any prisoner who happened to wander too close to the *'Dead Line'*, the interior 'no man's land' log barricade.

The newest, healthiest and strongest prisoners were always assigned to the burial detail. They were marched at gunpoint outside the stockade to an interment ground a hundred or so yards away. There numerous acres of earth was chewed-up and well turned over where several thousand bodies lay no more than a couple feet below the surface decomposing and disappearing with the final facts of their demise lost to their families and friends forever.

Joshua was aware that one of the long-time prisoners was trying to keep a record of the dead and the order of their deaths on scraps of paper he was able to find. He had passed the word around that should he die, someone must retrieve the account and pass it on until it could be documented by the Union authorities when the hostilities ended. That prisoner knew well, and without fear, that should he be caught with the records he would be hung or shot summarily. Those prisoners still able were self-assured that the Union would prevail against the Rebellion and so it became a common sentiment that the records must survive.

Joshua and the other prisoner carried the stiffening bodies of the hung, one by one, to the edge of the graves that loomed dark and empty and far too shallow. There were no blankets to wrap the dead and no coffin or markers to denote where the departed lay forgotten into eternity. They were still warm and he could smell the urine odor from between their legs. They were heavy, dead weight. The hoods had been removed, probably saved for the next unfortunate victim to be hanged or shot. Joshua tried not to look but couldn't help but see that their eyes were open and staring into, he guessed, that great mysterious void. But those dead eyes seemed to be following his every movement. He was conscious that fresh blood from the corpses had dribbled onto his hands and clothing. And he could smell it. It smelled of fear. It was that same smell he'd noticed after cornering a terrified farm animal and finally killing it. It was always as if the animal knew or sensed what was about to happen. Joshua often thought that on those occasions he could see fear or even a form of pleading in the animal's darting eyes.

Joshua and the other prisoner lowered the bodies as gently as they could into the holes. The sun was up and full now and both men sweated in the heat, their hands sore from the digging but toughened and unblistered after weeks of burials. Joshua grimaced at the thought of tossing dirt onto the faces of the dead men. Both dead men had been stripped of their clothing as it had become too valuable to squander on the departed. Dead men's clothing and belongings were passed around to those in need.

The two dead men lay on their backs staring up at Joshua and the other prisoner as dirt began to cover their faces.

"Should 'a closed their eyes," Joshua said.

The other prisoner nodded. "Say the usual words?"

"I reckon," Joshua said. He'd repeated the same words over every grave they'd dug. "Dear Lord, we commit these here men to you. Take care of their souls. They were good men and died fighting for their country. These here fellas were created by the hand of God and destroyed by the hand of man. Rest in peace. God bless Abraham Lincoln and our United States. Amen."

The other prisoner made the sign of the Cross and said, "Amen."

The guards snickered at Joshua's words. He stood and stared. The other prisoner threw down his shovel and walked toward the sneering guards. Joshua raised his hand.

"Billy, forget it. Let it go."

"I ain't put 'in up with this horse shit no more, Corporal." With that he spit into the face of the nearest guard. Rifle butts swung and bayonets flashed. In seconds Billy Smyth laid bloodied and still, his damaged face buried in the fresh muck, his ears bleeding and blood soaking his beard and matted hair. The gash in his throat continued squirting fine jets of crimson onto the chewed up muck and then slowly diminished and stopped. The attacking guards abruptly stood unspoken and still, staring blankly at the pathetic remains of their impulsive and brutal attack. The guard wiped his face and then turned and walked toward the stockade. The others used their bayonets to prod Joshua. He began to strip the clothing off Billy Smyth's still warm body. One guard picked up a shovel and jammed it in the dirt indicating where Joshua was to dig another grave. "Plant that Sumbitch here," he said, and then he opened his trousers and urinated on the spot, grinning at his comrades.

Joshua looked into the lifeless eyes of Billy Smyth. The guards had kicked dirt onto Billy Smyth's distorted face. The dirt and the blood was coagulating into a muddle of revolting seep. Joshua bent down and using the dead man's shirt wiped the blood and dirt from his face.

"Damned fool," he whispered. "But I won't forget this."

CHAPTER THIRTEEN

The Escape

Sleepless nights crept up on Joshua and as the days and weeks wore on he became more and more unable to rest. Curled up in what was left of a tattered woolen army blanket on the bare, often damp earth, left him chilled, feverish and weak. Each day he discovered new festering sores on his body. His feet were cracked and foul and the toe nails were infected and coming off. He began to plan an escape. Appraisal of his circumstances left him to believe that the only route of escape was in the burying details that were still being handed out to him and a few others. But he was growing weaker by the day and realized that his days as a grave digger were numbered and he knew that if he was going to escape it had to be soon. The weather was changing and the frequency of thunder storms was increasing leaving the prisoners wet and chilled. The only advantage to the storms was that they helped to flush out the sewage and debris that was dumped daily into the sluggish Stockade creek.

The constant lack of food, fresh water and the relentless pestilence was killing the inmates in record numbers. When the wind was right, or actually wrong, the odor from the burial field was overpowering. The dead, buried in too shallow of graves, often thrust body parts up through the soil, and especially after rain storms, exposing them to prowling animals who would then dig up the rest of the corpse, gorging themselves on the rotting flesh. Rats, as big as house cats, roamed the field digging and eating what was left by the forest carnivores. The graves, left shallow because the prisoners were too weak to dig deep trenches, were such that the frequency of burials would have exhausted vigorous men. Burial parties, including Joshua, would daily witness prisoners vomiting the green bile from the unending hollow of vacant stomachs at the sight and odor of the exposed human relics. In time the burial parties gave up trying to rebury the remains and did the best they could to cover their noses and eyes to the absurd mental and physical invasion of the doom and fate of this pitiless killing field.

Joshua began to survey his surroundings each time he was sent out on a burial detail. He noted that the new gravesites were inching closer and closer toward a heavily forested area. The hundred feet tall pine trees that edged the growing cemetery were footed at the ground level with a myriad of berry bushes, saplings, and weed-like growths. Joshua thought that if the guards could be distracted even momentarily he might be able to make a dash for the woods and into the cover of the brush and trees before the guards could rally and shoot him.

The number of assigned burial detail guards was declining almost daily due to Robert E. Lee's need for fresh bodies to fling into the terminal clash with General Grant's Armies. Meanwhile the inmate population of the prison was growing steadily despite the inevitable daily deaths. Joshua selfishly coveted the clothing of the dead Billy Smyth in hopes that he could keep himself warmer with the extra clothing and begin to conserve his energy and health in order to have the strength needed to make his run toward freedom. He began to feel that death at the hands of the burial detail guards would be better that rotting and dying in Andersonville Prison. Most days while burying the recently dead, Joshua would look about the killing field and wonder if there was a 'hot-spot' somewhere nearby where his own remains would eventually lay rotting and forgotten.

Joshua decided that he would go alone. Thinking that if he made a run for it during a burial detail he would most likely be killed or in the least wounded, he didn't want to put any other prisoners in jeopardy. And, even if just wounded during a prison break and captured, the commander imposed standard punishment was hanging, or if he felt Christian that day, mercifully the firing squad. As the days and weeks wore on the burial field grew nearer and nearer to the edge of the forest. Joshua, against his sense of pride, loafed as much as possible during the grave digging in order to conserve his strength. Occasionally an annoyed guard would prod him with the point of a bayonet to get moving. He always protested that he was hungry and weak. This only drew sneers and resentment from the guards. He was very aware that the other grave diggers resented his lack of effort but likely suspected that he might be planning an escape. Even so, not one of the other diggers so much as eluded to his uncharacteristic change in conduct. Mostly they watched and wondered. They often could be seen whispering among themselves but their suspicions or pondering went no further.

The day before his planned break to freedom Joshua removed a reasonably decent pair of much holed boots from one of the dead prisoners being readied for burial. The boots were high-top cavalry style but unfortunately a size or two too big and with most of the heal missing from the right boot and with small holes in the soles of both boots. With nothing left of his socks to insulate his feet from the boots, Joshua would have to make do with bare skin against leather.

Occasionally when he felt it necessary to examine his feet he would pull the boots of at night only to discover that bits of his skin came away with the leather. His toenails had mostly disappeared. Usually there was areas of dried and tacky blood on his feet. The stink of his feet was nearly intolerable. Recently he had begun treating the open sores on his chest and legs with sap from dead and dying trees, hoping that the juice would somehow aid healing. His body hadn't felt the touch of soap and water for weeks and areas on his body were beginning to turn black with imbedded grime. His beard and hair were both shoulder-length and matted with dirt a myriad of odoriferous forms of camp debris. Three days after Joshua took the boots two significant things happened; the sole on his right boot came loose and two burial detail prisoners made a desperate run for the woods after throwing their shovels at the guards.

Oscar Hale, Private, Company C, First Massachusetts Infantry, died in a hail of bullets just at the edge of the woods. Private Frederick Coombs, Company E, Third Volunteer Pennsylvania Cavalry fell just inside the tree line shot through both legs. Frederick Coombs was hung without ceremony the following morning. They sat him on a chair because of his broken legs and two soldiers hosted him into the air with the noose tight around his neck. He hung there convulsing cruelly for minutes before he expired unmoving and silent in the rain. The colonel drew his revolver and fired one shot into the heart of the corpse. Joshua was selected to lead the burial party. Chosen again to bury a dead Union soldier in the rain and the mud.

For the next few days the rain continued but the daily burials never ceased and the digging parties struggled out to their somber duties every morning. They waded in ankle deep mud and the incessant rain did its best to expose decaying bodies to the frenzied elements and it wasn't difficult to see, during early morning burials while the light was still weak, the sun refusing to show, that some of the exposed flesh from the dead seemed to glow with a luminous light. Some of the prisoners began calling this phenomenon *Satan's Glow*. They each prayed in their own way for full light to arrive when the ghost-like flush seemed to fade into the sodden soil.

Joshua awakened stiff and cold. His ragged wool army blanket was damp and there was a layer of mud beneath his body but the rain had stopped and there was a hint of sun peeking just above the eastern wall of the stockade. The *Dead Line* stood there still and solemn, begging him in it's own way to come to him. He could visualize the *Dead Line* opening its arms to him more and more frequently. There were days when he actually considered embracing those ominous outreaching arms. Joshua thought about the 'call' of the *Line* and then put it out of his mind. His first thought was that he had to go. To wait any longer would insure his failure. Weaker by the day and growing skeletal thin he knew his strength was waning and another week, or maybe even another day, would be too long. His memory of the shooting of the escapees weighed heavily on his mind. The brutal hanging of the seriously wounded Private Coombs was too difficult to contemplate. If his escape attempt should fail he hoped, no he prayed, that he too would die quickly in a hail of gunfire. He had already managed to scribble a note on a wind-blown scrap of paper to be sent to his family after his death and secured it with one of the newest and healthiest prisoners. There was a chance that the war would be over soon and this late-comer to Andersonville Prison might survive. Meetings had been secretly held amongst the prisoners and it was agreed, no mandated, that if any should survive this man-made hell they would devote their lives to telling the world about the horrors and abuse suffered at the hands of the Confederate Criminals.

Joshua hoped that he would be assigned again to direct a burial detail for those that had surrendered in the night. Lately he had made efforts to walk tall and appear strong and energetic but each day this ruse became more and more difficult. He knelt and prayed next to his lean-to shelter, "Please Lord, just one more day."

As usual there was nothing to eat on this chilly and damp morning. The rumor was that the Confederacy was weakening and that any food supplies that existed were being shipped to the troops at the various fronts. Joshua went to the stream, now called Latrine River by the prisoners, and reluctantly washed his face and hands and drank just enough of the polluted water to fend off dehydration. Then he walked to a designated area of the stockade and urinated. He was thankful that the diarrhea that had plagued him for several days seemed to have subsided. On his way back to his lean-to he saw three armed soldiers approaching and shouting. They were forming a burial detail and assigning diggers. Joshua risked rejection by raising his hand in order that they would spot him for sure. They did. The guards shook their heads as if to say this one is ruined. They scowled and began to ignore him Joshua stepped up, ready to go.

"You there, Yankee Shit, ya'll too scrawny to be dig 'in anymore. Git the hell out of the way." The other guards laughed, shaking their heads.

Joshua froze. "I ain't. I'm strong and I wanna help bury my dead brothers. And I wanna be able to say words over them."

One of the soldiers laughed as he prodded Joshua with his bayonet.

"Ya'll sure pick shit for brothers." He laughed. The other two joined in. One of the soldiers wore corporal's stripes on his butternut coat.

"Alright," he said, "git a couple of others and the shovels and picks. Double-quick. Ya'll got 3 stiff ones to plant. And git them planted before they start to stink...stink worse that is." Words that had become a common maxim.

The other two laughed again. Joshua felt the point of the bayonet in his sparse ribs. Another quarter inch and he'd be punctured, he thought, while attempting to pull away. The guard pushed stiffer with his bayonet, grinning.

"Hurry up," one of the soldiers said. "You Yanks smell even worse when ya'll's dead. If that's possible." More laughter from the three.

Joshua was wearing every piece of clothing he owned but he desperately wanted his blanket, or what was left of it, but there was no time. The three soldiers followed him toward his lean-to. The blanket was still spread on the ground where he had left it. He tried to pick it up as he passed the lean-to. The corporal prodded him with his bayonet, pushing him slightly past his shelter.

"You don't need that flea-bag-rag." One guard held his nose and faked a gag.

"I'm kind 'a cold, Corporal," Joshua said.

"You'll git warm dig 'in," the corporal said. "Git your diggers and let's go."

"But I could wrap it around my shoulders," Joshua said.

"Naw," the corporal said, "you might try to run off if ya have that there rag. Damn things full of lice anyways. Maybe even a rat in there. Rat turds for sure." More laughter from the three guards.

Joshua was alarmed. Were they expecting him to make a run for it? Had another prisoner who'd heard the rumor that Joshua was going to make a break let it be known. There was suspicion that the Rebs had planted spies amongst the prisoners. But it was doubtful. The word around camp was that a Reb soldier would have to be an insane patriot to submit himself to the tortures of being inside the stockade at Andersonville Prison.

"You hear me, Yank?" the guard yelled.

"Yeah," Joshua said, "and freeze or starve to death in them there woods, or maybe even be shot by you Rebs. No thanks."

Since the death of Sergeant Hall Joshua considered himself the leader of a small group of prisoners that had voluntarily attached themselves to him. The three ignored him. Joshua yelled to two of the newest and healthiest prisoners and ordered them to join in. Reluctantly they crawled out of their lean-tos and joined the burial party walking toward a log hut area where the dead bodies had been stacked by the guards. Make-shift stretchers were laying nearby and Joshua and the others loaded the first body and walked toward the burial ground. At the gate a pair of guards slid the entrance open and the funeral party proceeded toward the burial grounds.

The corporal walked to a spot near the edge of the forest and instructed Joshua to begin digging. The three guards then seemed to relax. Joshua noticed that they were leaning on their muskets. Two of the guards rolled cigarettes and began smoking. Their conversation was muffled but Joshua could hear enough to know they were discussing the war news. The nature of the conversation was that the South was struggling to maintain an army worthy of putting up a fight. The corporal began talking about what he was planning to do after the war. Joshua made passive glances toward the tree-line 15 or 20 yards away. He also noted that the corporal was standing close enough to be struck by a shovel if it became necessary, or actually, if the opportunity arose. Joshua held the faint hope that if he attack the guards the other two prisoners would join in the fight. Joshua wanted to escape and travel alone but he'd not mind if the others made a run for freedom along with him. Three men running provided more targets for the shooters but also increased the possibility that he would not be hit. A flesh wound while escaping would probably kill him within a few days following the seemingly requisite green running puss that almost always developed in flesh wounds or those that shattered bones. He feared another head wound, one that might leave him wandering aimlessly until he perished or was captured.

As Joshua helped dig the graves his mind wandered to home and he pondered what his mother was doing at this very moment and he imagined what Katie Hespeth might be doing. Did she think about him or had she forgotten him and their plans for the future. Had one of the other young men in the area taken up with Katie. Had one of those stay-at-home shirkers taken advantage of his absence? Shirkers? Maybe those young men were smarter than him. Maybe they were home eating a hot farm breakfast of ham and eggs and drinking coffee with cream. And…those boys weren't digging graves on a damp morning at Andersonville Prison being watched over by three Confederate guards who would like nothing more than to shoot him dead.

Was Joshua Cole stupid, he asked himself? Stupid to have left home? Stupid to have left Katie Hespeth as fair game to all those shirkers? He looked at the tree line. Time to go. Then he looked at the morning sky. The sky was growing dark with threatening clouds. Were the clouds a bad omen? Were the clouds a warning? He kept digging and taking furtive glances toward the guards. They were still leaning on their muskets and talking. Then it began to rain. First with fat scattered drops and then with increasing intensity. Despair crowded into Joshua's mind. He felt his stomach begin to crawl and his arms and hands started trembling.

Suddenly one of the other prisoners screamed and threw his shovel at the guards and made a break for the tree-line. The guards snapped up their guns and fired almost in unison. The running prisoner stumbled, staggered and then fell face down at the very edge of the trees. Joshua was stunned at the abruptness of the violence and apparent sudden death, but quickly realized that now was his chance to go. The three guards had fired their single-shot rifles and wouldn't be able to shoot. The sudden impulse of the prisoner to make a run for freedom was the break Joshua needed. Without a second's indecision he threw his shovel at the three guards and ran for the tree-line.

Twenty feet from the trees Joshua tripped over the dying prisoner and fell. A guard quickly over-took him and began yelling obscenities and waving his bayonet threateningly. Joshua looked into the eyes of the guard and saw something there, something unidentifiable. He tried to discern the anomaly, was it sadness, fear, hate or fatigue? He was the only guard that had given chase while the others were frantically reloading their guns. Sickened, Joshua put his hands in the air as a sign of surrender. Then the guard suddenly removed the bayonet from Joshua's chest, stepped back, nodded and pointed the bayonetted rifle toward the trees.

"Go on Yank," he said. "Be quick about it."

Joshua was startled. He gradually lowered his hands.

"What?"

"Go on gawd damn it, before they git loaded."

Joshua rolled onto his feet and without haste stumbled into the trees.

At once he heard yelling that sounded like the soldier that had let him go was catching verbal hell from his companions. Once into the cover of the trees he ran stumbling and tripping over vines and dead wood and within moments heard shots being fired wildly into his path. One bullet came close clipping leaves and branches out of a tree just over his head. He began to zigzag back and forth hoping that one of those assorted wild shots would not hit him. Quickly the shooting stopped as the guards emptied their single shot muskets.

Joshua's legs wobbled as if his knees were made of bread dough. He repeatedly fell, only to struggle back to his feet to fall again. With his lungs burning and stressed for air he ran aimlessly into a sudden clearing in the woods and wholly out of control, pitched head first down a steep embankment into a small stream. He was in the water for only a moment before he gathered himself and was out and up the opposite bank and running for the woods. Once into the trees he dove into a bramble of bushes and lay gasping for air. It was only then that he realized he had gashed his forearm badly in one of his falls. He lay there trying to access his condition. He was soaked clear through and he was aware that his right ankle hurt and that the sole of his boot had come loose and was hanging by no more that a thread. He looked around surveying his surroundings and listening for any sounds that might indicate he was being pursued.

CHAPTER FOURTEEN

Bat (The Slave)

Several hours later Joshua found himself confronted with the aspect of a long cold and wet night without the benefit of cover nor anything to eat. His ankle had begun to swell soon after his escape. The blood on his forearm had congealed, but it was swollen and painful. He was still wet from the plunge into the stream and the incessant rain that had persisted throughout the day. He knew that he was still very deep in Rebel Territory and if spotted he would most likely be shot or in the least captured and returned to Andersonville Prison for an early morning rendezvous with the hangman's noose or a firing squad.

Just before dark of this third day of walking and hiding Joshua found himself on the outskirts of what appeared to be a plantation or what was left of a plantation. In the distance he could see a manor of sorts surrounded by outbuildings, a large barn-like structure and stables. Moss hung shawl-like from dozens of Valley Oaks surrounding the grounds proper. He was acutely aware that smoke drifted up lazily into the misting gloom and that someone was in that house and enjoying the warmth of a fire or cooking the evening meal. He guessed that the small cottage-like outbuildings were slave quarters and the barn a storage center for tobacco or cotton or both. He knew, and had known for a long time, that cotton was king in the southern states. The house itself appeared to be brick with a large surrounding covered porch and rather large windows in both the upstairs and downstairs. A stone walkway, guarded by the statue of a black stable-boy, lead from the cobble-stone drive to the steps leading onto the veranda. Double entrance doors offered a grand entrance into the manor house and what appeared to be a ship's brass bell hung near the door as a sounder for arriving guests. Just to the right of the bell a ships' wheel hung ceremoniously attached to the brick wall causing Joshua to wonder if this plantation master made his fortune in shipping or was a wealthy retired ship's captain.

Sitting there in the dripping trees he wondered if he might creep in amongst the outbuildings and find a place to spend the night and maybe something to eat in a corn crib or smoke house, a blanket, or some clothes. He sat shivering until full dark had descended and the house and outbuildings were no longer in view but lights twinkled in the dark and the wonderful smell of wood smoke began to drift his way.

He sat alone thinking about his former life. He thought about Katie Hespeth and about his mother. He wondered how Sergeant Dan Kelly was doing and hoped that he was still fighting the Rebellion. He wished he had one of Kelly's cigars to smoke, and more over wished he was with Kelly. Sergeant Kelly was safety. Sergeant Kelly was strength. He considered Daniel Kelly his friend and sort of a mentor and hoped that Kelly knew that, although Joshua had never had the nerve to tell him.

Hours later the twinkling manor lights went out and Joshua felt it was safe to begin creeping down the hillside toward the plantation. His shivering had grown worse and any attempt to quell it failed. The rain had stopped but everything was wet and dripping and the ground under his feet squished with every step. The sole of his right boot had finally come off leaving him limping on the swollen ankle and hurting his exposed sole on rocks and debris. He'd gone only a few yards when he heard a dog bark. He crouched in the darkness and waited, listening to see if he was going to be chased by angry plantation dogs. A half hour later the dog or dogs were still yapping. Joshua's shivering grew worse. Sitting beneath a dripping tree he began to wonder if he was going to be able to walk. His knees felt weak and wobbly. His stomach growled loud enough that he once looked around to see if a dog had found him. Then he heard a voice from the area of the manor house. It was a woman's voice and she was calling the dog or dogs in.

"Thank God," Joshua murmured aloud.

Then lights came on in the manor house. Joshua watched unmoving. In a few minutes the lights went out and the house was dark again. Then a light came on in one of the out-buildings and a door opened casting light out onto the grounds. A man came out and stood in the light of the door. A match flared as if he was lighting a pipe or cigar. From where Joshua sat the man appeared to be tall and broad. In a few minutes he went back inside and closed the door and the light went out. Joshua waited, giving the occupants time to fall asleep.

A half hour or so later he began his decent toward the buildings. As his strength faded each step became torment. Wobbling unevenly he began to search in the dark for a walking stick in order to keep himself upright. He found a five or six foot length of tree limb. He couldn't help but think the limb could serve as a weapon if needed.

It took Joshua a half an hour of staggering, falling and getting back up to reach the edge of the compound. He stopped and leaned against the wall of the first building he came to and listened. Then he moved on to the next building, the one that housed the big man. He listened and was certain he could hear snoring from within. Suddenly a light came on inside and in an instant the door opened and the large man stepped out into the light from the open doorway. Joshua froze. He could smell the man's sweat stained clothes and a remnant of tobacco smoke. He was no more than five feet from the door. The big man stood there quietly for a few minutes listening and looking about and then unbuttoned his trousers and urinated on the ground. Then Joshua heard him mumble something in a deep resonant voice and then go back inside closing the door. In a minute the light went out. Joshua sank to the ground sitting in inches deep mud, his face buried in his trembling hands. The big man was black and most likely a slave of some stature. He began to listen again for the snoring but was frustrated when after fifteen or twenty minutes there was nothing. He wondered if the big man was troubled about something and quietly listening. Fat rain drops began to pelt Joshua's head and shoulders.

Now increasingly desperate to find some sort of shelter for the night he crept past the hut and felt his way toward what appeared to be a barn or storage building. At the edge of the building he began running his hands along the wall until he felt what seemed to be a sliding wooden door of sorts and grasping the outer edge began pushing. The door started to slide open without sound and at once the familiar smell of hay and farm animals wafted out into the damp night air. For a short moment Joshua was back in the Conrad's barn on the night he had left home. Then forcing himself quickly to break the spell took careful steps into the gloom of the barn. A horse whinnied somewhere in the dark and stomped its hooves. He heard what sounded like pigeons or chickens fluttering high up in the rafters. Something scurried across the barn floor right in front of him. A barn rat, Joshua decided. He stood still while his eyes adjusted to the gloom. He hoped to find a hay loft or such where he could sleep for a few hours. The remnants of a ragged wool blanket he'd found in the woods was tied around his waist. It wasn't much more than a large rag but it was all he had and although wet it would have to do for cover and warmth. In the dark he found an empty stall with straw on the floor and laid down amidst the horse dropping wrapped in his blanket and went directly to sleep. In his slumber he dreamed of Andersonville Prison and the guard that had, for whatever reason, allowed him to flee into the trees and escape. Somehow Katie Hespeth was there in the prison with him and he kept trying to hide her from the other prisoners and desperately looking for a way to get her out. Every time he reached for her hand she faded into smoke and then drifted away into a darkening fog.

What seemed like only minutes later Joshua was awakened from an edgy slumber when a match flared nearby, paused momentarily while a lantern brightened and came to life. Through blinking eyes Joshua saw a huge black man staring at him. There was a lethal looking revolver shoved into the waistband of his trousers. He slowly moved his right hand to the butt of the revolver and shook his head slowly as if warning Joshua to remain still. Joshua raised both hands in surrender and let himself fall back into the hay. He was caught. Visions of Andersonville Prison and bodies hanging on hemp ropes from a dead tree crowded his consciousness.

"What's ya'll do'in here Suh?" the big man said.

Joshua just shook his head and stared into the gloom above him. He felt tears of frustration welling up in his eyes. It was over and…he had tried so hard; had spent so many days alone in the woods, and having left the others behind to what kind of fate he could only shudder at.

"Suh? The big man said again. The big man loomed large and foreboding there in the gloom of the barn. Joshua felt weak and defeated. There was no way he could compete with this giant. It was over.

"Hiding," Joshua said.

"Hid 'in from what?" the big man said.

Joshua struggled to his feet. The big man put his hand back on the butt of the revolver. Joshua could see him shaking his head as if a warning.

"Massuh, ya'll be slow 'bout git 'in up," the big man warned.

"Won't have any trouble with me," Joshua said. "I've had all the trouble I can handle."

The big man held the lantern closer to Joshua and examined him in the yellow glow, his eyes widening. Then he shook his head.

"You sick?"

"Some," Joshua said. "Ain't et much in weeks. Nothing for two, three days."

"You a yank?" the big man said. "Yankee soder?"

"Pennsylvania," Joshua said. "98th Pennsylvania, Company A."

"Is dem stripes on ya'll's coat?"

Joshua looked down at what was left of his sack coat. The corporal stripes were so faded they had nearly vanished. He sat back down in the hay. His legs couldn't hold him upright any longer. He felt dizzy and was nearly overcome with nausea. He needed to vomit. He leaned to one side and gagged but nothing came up but green bile. The big man watched, shaking his head.

"You is fo'sho sick, Massuh."

"Union Army," Joshua said. "I escaped from Andersonville Prison."

The big man took his hand off the butt of the revolver and smiled through his thick gray beard.

"Well God bless Abrim Limcoln," he said. "Ya'll gonna set us niggers free. Yessuh, ya'll boys and Abrim Limcoln gonna do it."

Joshua felt a slight surge of relief. Perhaps this giant black man was a Union Sympathizer.

The big man hung the lantern from a nail and sat down in the hay next to Joshua.

"What's you're name?" he said.

"Cole, Joshua Cole. Corporal."

"Well hello mister Corporal Cole," the big man said. "Welcome to Johnston Manor. Dis here my homes since I was borned."

Then the big man pulled off his coat and draped it around Joshua's shoulders.

"You shake' in sum bad Corporal Cole," he said. "Real wet and doan smells too good. Dats for sure."

"So what do they call you by?" Joshua asked.

"Theys call me Bat. I'm Bat Johnston. I's taken my massuh's name same as the other niggers he'ah."

"You a slave, Bat?"

Bat laughed softly. "Now what you think Corporal Cole? What's I look like?"

"Well?"

"Yes'suh. I bin a slave for Massuh Johnston since I was borned on dis here plantation. Me and he was jus pups together in the beginning. But I's a boss slave now and help keep the other niggers in line. Bat's sum'thin special Massuh Johnston say. He say Bat he strong as a mule. And then he say he as ugly as one too. That Massuh Johnston likes to tease old Bat. He a colonel now in the army. Me an Missy sure do miss him."

Joshua's stomach rolled and he gagged but resisted vomiting. He could taste the green bile in his mouth and had to spit into the hay.

"Bat Johnston do you think I might git something to eat and to drink?"

"First I's gotta tell Missy Savannah you is hid' in in this barn."

Joshua shook his head. He felt fear and bile rise in his throat.

"Do you gotta do that, Bat?" Joshua remembered hearing a woman's voice calling a dog. "And where's the dog, or dogs?"

"The dog he is older than them hills and he ain't got much teeth. He no worry to you, Corporal Cole. His name is Thumper 'cause of his noisy tail wag' in just all the time agin the wall or da door. Missy Savannah? I 'Pose I should tell her about you, see'in as I's a boss nigger and Massuh Johnston away to the war. Missy Savannah she all alone now 'cause her momma dun gone to be wit da Lord. God bless Lady Johnston. Lady Johnston she was try 'in to birth a new baby but the child won't come out. Theys buried over yonder in the med'a. Dug da hole and carved da cross my'sef."

Bat looked toward the roof of the barn as if he was waiting to be accepted by a higher up.

"She'll have me arrested and sent back to Andersonville."

Bat shook his big head.

"Missy Savannah is a sweet, sweet lady and she'll unnerstan."

"She an old lady?" Joshua asked.

Bat laughed quietly. "Oh no, Missy Savannah she young and pretty. So pretty."

"But she'll have me arrested."

"Wrong, Corporal Cole," Bat said, "she'll watch over you 'til you is well enough."

"No she won't," Joshua said. "She's a Rebel woman and they hate all us Yanks. She hates you slaves too."

"No suh," Bat said. "Missy Savannah is a sweet lady and she dun't hate no ones. Not even ya'll yanks. Fact is I held Missy Savannah when she's jus' a tiny baby. Missy loves her big ole' Bat. Missy sometimes minds me my lil' girl. She gone to da Lord lang time ago from da fever."

Bat put his hand on the pistol and smiled through his beard.

"Dis gun here is broke. Now you stay here and I's be back shortly."

Joshua lay back in the hay with resignation. No longer could he run. He was finished. His body and spirit drained. He lay there in the hay feeling like a whipped dog and thinking that just maybe he would have been better off had the prison guards shot him. Joshua tried to sleep for the next few hours. Bat's coat had brought him some much needed cover and warmth. Lying in the hay he could smell the scent of Bat Johnston and felt that it was not all that unpleasant and that somehow the presence of it comforted him.

The morning sky was beginning to lighten when coatless Bat returned to the barn. Joshua had finally managed to doze some but his shivering and persistent hunger kept him restless and fretful. Bat's heavy coat had continued to help hold off the early morning chill, and Joshua wondered if Bat Johnston had set himself up for a cold morning without his coat. The big man carried a basket and a crockery jug. He sat down in the hay next to Joshua and smiled while opening the basket. The first thing out of the basket was a bulky wool blanket.

"Nows you gotta go slow on dis here vittles. Thems make ya sick real quick."

"She coming?" Joshua said, shaking his head and looking straight into Bat's the eyes.

Bat handed Joshua a chicken leg and a large piece of cornbread.

"Hush a bit while ya eat sum'thin, Corporal Cole."

Bat poured cider into a crockery cup and sat it next to Joshua. Joshua picked up the cup and drank the entire contents.

"Ya'll go slowly," Bat said.

Joshua put the cup down and pointed at it craving a refill.

"Well did you tell her?"

"Missy Savannah just getting up now. I's tell her later."

Then Joshua turned away from Bat, gagged, and vomited into the hay. Bat shook his head, reached over and held Joshua's shoulders.

"I's told ya so, Corporal Cole. You a hard head."

After another half hour Joshua was able to eat and keep it down. Bat sat in the hay smoking his pipe and watching Joshua.

"Shouldn't be smoking in this hay," Joshua said.

Bat grinned. "I's careful to smoke in da barn. Missy Savannah don't likes it one little bit dat I smoke, so's I's gotta hide out mos' da time. Her daddy smokes cigars but Missy don't dare say nuthin to Massuh Johnston 'bout it. Massuh Johnston he dun't take no guff from nobody never. Massuh Johnston he a Colonel now in the Army of Nort Virginy. He fight 'in along wit his brother, General Joe."

Joshua looked up from his chicken leg. "General Joe Johnston?"

"Yes' sir. Dats him. Big mean old Joe Johnston. I's knows him well."

"Bat, why don't you just runaway and join the Union Army? General Grant is taking colored folks now so's they can help fight for their freedom."

Bat shook his head. "My head's bin work' in on dat some but I's love Missy Savannah and all her fambly. Missy one time stop da foreman from whup'in old Bat wit da horse whip. Dat foreman he done gone to da Lord. If da Lord would have him."

"Why were they whipping you?"

Bat looked away and avoided Joshua's eyes.

"Bat, why'd they whip you?"

"'Cause old Bat got too friendly whit one of da slave girls and she sort 'a da property of da foreman."

"The foreman a white man?"

"Yessuh. Him white as snow, 'cept he a dirty man. The slave girls say he one mean Sumbitch. Fo'given the word. Please."

"The foreman having knowledge of the slave girl?"

Bat looked away.

"Yessuh. Most'im. My sweetheart wit child."

"This slave girl, did you like her?"

"Yessuh. I did so very much."

"Did she want to be with Bat?"

"That she say," Bat said.

"Is the child yours, Bat?"

Bat looked away again.

"No'suh. Dat child is da foreman's through no do'in of hers."

"Why didn't you kill the bastard?"

Bat smiled, shrugged his massive shoulders and puffed his pipe. Looked away toward the barn door.

"Bat?"

Bat frowned this time and then groaned deep in his chest, looked around the barn as if fearful someone might be listening and spoke in a mere whisper.

"Yessuh, but da Lord dun it for me. Yes he did."

"What's her name?" Joshua said.

"When she born Massuh Johnston name her his self."

"Her name?"

"Jasmine. Yessuh, my sweet little Jasmine. Pretty as flower."

"Take your shirt off, Bat," Joshua said.

"Suh?"

"Take your shirt off and turn around. Please!"

"Dun cold here in da barn, Corporal Cole."

Bat stood up slowly and unbuttoned the three buttons that were left on his shirt front and slowly took the shirt off and then stood looking at Joshua. Joshua saw the massive power in Bat's shoulders and arms. His forearms were corded and veined, his hands thick and calloused.

"Turn around," Joshua said.

Bat slowly turned around. Joshua frowned and looked away. Bat's back and shoulders were lined and crossed like a road map with healed welts from a whip or cane. Some of the marks had faded to white with age.

"The foreman?" Joshua said.

"Dun't matter any," Bat said.

"Missy, what's her name? Charlotte? Didn't stop him often enough?"

Bat turned around and began putting his shirt back on. Joshua saw a darkening look in Bat's eyes. Joshua began feel he had blundered with his attitude.

"Her name Savannah and she not round all da times dat foreman whup'in Bat. Missy gone way to school some times up nort."

"School? Naw, she too busy being a Southern Belle?"

Joshua quickly realized he quickly blundered again.

Bat's expression changed and he took a step toward Joshua. Joshua leaned away.

Bat stood glaring down at Joshua, his eyes dark and slightly squinted.

"Corporal Cole, no cause you be mouth 'in Missy Savannah."

Joshua put his hand out to shake. Bat took it in his massive right hand, the dark fading from his eyes. Joshua could feel the calluses and power.

"I am sorry Bat Johnston, I didn't mean to hurt you."

"You be easy wit Missy, she dun lost her husband-to-be in dat awful war. He been dead more 'in a haft year now. Missy..., God bless her, she don't cry no more 'bout it. Nows I be on my way. I's work to do. And I's talk to Missy about this here Union Soder sleep' in in her barn."

The third morning after Joshua had been discovered; he awakened just as the sky was beginning to lighten. He had made a decision that he would ask Bat for some provision and then leave in an attempt to get back to his own regiment in the north. He had no idea where he would find the troops and Sergeant Kelly but he knew that he had to get moving soon. The thought had passed through his mind that he might be considered a deserter. Hopefully there were others that had witnessed his capture by the enemy that could validate his disappearance for so many months. And he wanted to be gone before being discovered by this 'Savannah person' or others. He truly believed that any loyal southerner would turn him over to the authorities the minute he was exposed. He was concerned that if that happened things would not go well for Bat. Southern forgiveness would be scarce in light of his aiding and abetting the enemy. Bat Johnston would truly be fortunate to receive only the whip in lieu of a hangman's noose or bullet.

CHAPTER FIFTEEN

Savannah Johnston

An hour later Joshua's reverie was suddenly broken by voices. The outwardly cautious voice of Bat Johnston came muted through the thin walls of the barn and Joshua was sure he noticed a slight tremor in place of the usual baritone pitch. Then a female voice emerged out of the early gloom and Joshua began to look for an escape route out of the barn. It was too late. The sliding door opened swiftly and he heard the female say, "Well Battis, where is he?"

Joshua struggled to conceal himself. Visions of Andersonville Prison flashed through his mind. He saw an image of himself swinging at the end of a hangman's noose; heard the sound of rifle fire as he was executed before a firing squad; felt the impact of bullets in his chest and saw the red-fire burst before his eyes as he toppled toward the earth.

A match flared and a lantern came to life. Joshua was suddenly aware of his neglected person; weeks of filth and stench, bearded, ragged and worse yet…his facial features most likely revealing a visage of panic and terror. Failing to crawl into the hay mound Joshua pulled the wool blanket around his face. Shuffling footsteps approached and the blanket was silently lifted off. At the same moment he heard the barn door being slid shut and heard Bat say, "Is ya'll sure Missy?" Then Bat was gone, but Joshua was not alone. He was startled when someone sat down in the hay next to him with the lantern held high. The pleasant scent of lilac filled his consciousness, wholly cleansing the smell of barn and animals. He sensed warmth emanating from the body next to him. She sat there in the hay in the lantern light looking directly at him. Then she reached to the blanket and gently wrapped it around his shoulders, leaned back and shook her head.

"You're chilled," she said.

Joshua realized he was trembling.

Then she reached and brushed the hair away from his forehead.

"Ain't you a sight," she said softly. "You've a nasty looking scar on your forehead. And that blond hair is matted something terrible. You could use a shave and a hair cut."

"Reb bullet," Joshua said, fingering the thick scar. "Ya'll angry with Bat? Ain't his fault you know?"

"No Yank, I'm not," she said. "Bat is just a great big child. He'd help a stray kitten or pup…or even a stray Yank."

"I ain't no stray Miss," Joshua said, "I'm a corporal in the Army of the United States and I've escaped from your Andersonville Prison."

She drew her hand away. "Isn't my prison," she said.

Savannah sat back looking directly into his eyes. Joshua knew he had erred. Then she smiled lightly and shook her head.

"Bat gave me away, didn't he?" Joshua said.

"Oh my goodness Yank, I seen Battis traipsing off with baskets of vittles. Don't you think I was curious?"

"Well?"

"And one of my best wool blankets. C'mon Yank. I'm not some dumb southern belle as you might think. Battis told me that you think I'm spending my days being the Belle of Johnston Manor."

"I didn't say that," Joshua said, avoiding her eyes. She took a deep exasperated breath. Joshua ventured a look at her.

"Yank?" She stared straight into his eyes.

Joshua cringed and looked away, not able to meet the potency of her eyes.

"Well maybe I thought it."

"Actually I'm spending my days trying to feed Battis…now you."

"Your slave folks gone?" Joshua said.

"All except Bat. You haven't heard about Mister Lincoln's Emancipation Proclamation?" Savannah said.

"His what?"

"Emancipation Proclamation…it frees the slaves."

"He did that?" Joshua said.

"Yes, you Yanks think you know how everyone should live. My family has farmed with slaves for a hundred or more years. Battis and his people don't know anything else. What gave Mister Lincoln the right to do that?"

Joshua couldn't find an answer.

"Savannah? That's your name?"

"Yes it is," Savannah said, "my Daddy was born in Savannah, Georgia and named me after his home town. Savannah Marie. Marie is my Momma's name. She's buried in the meadow with my baby sister."

"I know about that," Joshua said. "I know about your loss in the war, too. I'm sorry."

"Bat talks too much," Savannah said, looking away. She looked back at Joshua, he thought he saw moisture in her eyes.

Joshua nodded. "Georgia is not my favorite state."

"And you are Joshua Cole. Corporal Joshua Cole."

"Joshua David Cole…at your service."

"Looks like I'm at your service, "Savannah said. "Where are you from? Joshua David Cole"

"Hanover, Pennsylvania. Farm. Just a farm boy."

With that statement Joshua remembered Corporal Homan and felt a loss. He could hear once again Homan yelling something like, "Farm Boy, you're the worse of the worse."

Savannah got up to leave, brushing the hay from her riding pants and long-tailed shirt. She wore a pair of riding boots that reached to her knees. Her eyes had cleared. She saw him inspecting her clothing.

"Daddy's," she said. "I've been to Pennsylvania. Fact is I went to school there for two years just before this awful war started. I've got work to do."

Joshua looked up at her and shook his head.

"Do you have to? I mean right now? Your hair is beautiful." Then thinking, there I go embarrassing my self again.

Savannah scowled and shook her head.

"It's not! And yes. I'll send Battis out with some breakfast for you."

"Thank you, Miss Johnston."

"It's Savannah, not miss Johnston. And you need a bath. Battis will fetch you some hot water and clean clothes."

"I prefer to wear my uniform," Joshua said. "Or what's left of it."

"Suit yourself," Savannah said, "but it needs washing. Take your clothes off."

Joshua looked down at himself.

"What?"

Savannah smiled. "I won't watch. Take your clothes off. Use the blanket to cover up."

"Not in front of you," Joshua said.

"Oh Joshua David Cole I've seen naked men before."

"Not me," Joshua said.

"Suppose you have something different? I'll send Battis."

"What kind 'a man you seen naked? Then said to himself, "Cole, shut up."

Savannah raised her eyes toward the roof.

"Well that's none of your business Joshua David Cole."

Savannah turned and walked toward the barn door.

"Miss Savannah," Joshua said.

Savannah stopped and turned. "Yes?"

"Can you come back?"

"Depends," Savannah said over her shoulder, "if you think you can be a gentleman...and forget about that *Belle of the South thing.*"

"I can sure do that," Joshua said. "Yes I can."

Savannah turned and walked away. She paused at the barn door and gave a sudden cautious glance back over her shoulder as a strand of hair fell across her eyes. A fleet but skillful toss of her head solved the problem and she disappeared through the barn door into the morning gloom. The barn felt colder and darker after Savannah was gone. He could still smell the lilac scent of her. He tried to make it linger but it soon faded and the barn scent returned shoddier than ever.

Joshua took off his filthy uniform and tied it in a bundle. The dead soldier's boots were in tatters. He threw them into a corner. Possibly Bat could find him something to wear on his feet. He knew he needed to leave and get back to his own army and for the journey he would need shoes or boots. Sitting back in the hay wrapped in Savannah's wool blanket he decided that maybe he should stay for a few more days to recover the strength he would need for the walk north. Somehow he found it easy to want to stay.

He lay back in the hay and began to think about Savannah Johnston's physical features. Mostly he thought he prized her abundance of auburn hair, full and reaching down to the middle of her back and he'd been alert enough to notice how the arc of the lantern light had reflected sun-shine highlights along its length. But in retrospect he decided, after considerable contemplation, that her large brown eyes were her best feature, bright, intelligent, and they seemed to look right into you. The eyes were supported only by wonderfully high cheek-bones that enhanced her features and added a palpable strength to a striking face. He found himself thinking about her lips and shocked himself by seriously considering he would like to kiss them, and would if he ever got the chance. Not likely to happen, he supposed. Then he rebuked himself thinking 'Joshua Cole, don't get carried away about some 'Southern Belle.' Then he thought about the food she and Bat had been sending him and realized that Savannah Johnston looked too thin. Quickly he reached a disturbing insight, Savannah and Bat were giving him food they needed.

"Yes," he said aloud, "I'll stay awhile. But eat less. And not because of that girl." But wholly realized, while reproving himself, that she was the very reason he'd decided to stay longer.

In the days that followed visits from Savannah were infrequent and he lamented at the end of the days that he had not seen her. Every morning he awakened early and made desperate attempts to make himself presentable, in hopes that this would be one of her rare morning visits. On a few occasions Savannah had lingered and they had talked about their lives and their hopes for the future. Joshua had found himself cautiously avoiding any discussion of Katie Hespeth, but with Savannah's persistence had finally admitted to having a girl at home, but not a serious one for sure, he'd added.

Soon Joshua began to see his days in the barn at Johnston Plantation as halcyon and he was beginning to regret the idea, or the necessity, of his leaving and going back north to find his army. Day by day his health was improving and felt his strength returning. The open sores on his body were healing from the care Battis had provided using some kind of ointment that was used to heal the wounds of farm animals and even the slaves. He also knew he needed to write to his mother, and maybe even Katie, but somewhere deep in his emergent awareness he wanted to remain anonymous for the time being.

Something was shifting in his mind, something he could not readily identify. After a few days in the barn he began to speculate about the house and even hoped that eventually he would be invited in. At night, after dark, he often crept outside and sat in the gloom watching the house and wondering what Savannah might be doing at that very moment. He wondered which of the rooms was her bedroom and found himself thinking about her things. Many of her things would be in that bedroom, her clothes, her books, her very personal things. He imagined that somewhere in that room she had a picture of her lost fiancés and maybe a collection of his letters to her from the war. He envied that man, that dead Confederate soldier. Before his death he had held Savannah close, had felt the warmth of her body, tasted her lips, buried his face in her hair. His untimely death in this deplorable war had destroyed a life of bliss and had sadly cheated him of the many wonderful years he and Savannah would have shared. Joshua admitted to himself that if he ever got Savannah Johnston in his arms he would never let her go. Yes, he thought, what was it he'd read in a book by some ancient writer? Something about the mind going through a sudden *'sea change.'* A change to different thinking; unusual or uncommon thinking. Yes, this *sea change* thing was happening to him and he could not really discern why, or was it he didn't want to know why?

CHAPTER SIXTEEN

Rebel Cavalry

During the next few days Joshua looked forward to Savannah's rare visits to the barn and was always disappointed when the door slid open and there stood Bat smiling and holding a basket of food. It wasn't that he didn't like Bat, Bat had become, in a way, his Dark Knight. On two occasions Bat had smuggled a few of Colonel Johnston's cigars out of the house and they had bonded, in sorts, while smoking, talking, and listening for the footsteps of Savannah. Bat had warned that they were both in deep trouble if caught smoking. On one visit Savannah had sniffed the air, squinted suspiciously at both of them and left the barn, leaving Bat and Joshua wondering if they had angered her.

Morning sounds. Horses stomping; rooster crowing; the barn walls creaking and popping from early sun and then... voices of men. Struggling to arouse himself Joshua heard saddle leather creak and the faint jangle of metal. He opened his eyes into the early morning gloom of the barn. He pushed the blankets away, sat up and listened. The sounds were all too familiar. The sounds of army. The sounds of cavalry. Creaking leather, snorting horses, hooves pawing the earth. Muffled voices. The sound of the enemy. The barn door slid open. Joshua crawled back into the hay mound and began to pull straw over himself when he heard Bat's voice.

"Corporal Cole, theys Confederate Cavalry and theys got many Union boys wit'im. Dem boys in ropes and chains. Ya'll needs ta stay berry quiet 'til them Rebs leave.

"Battis, I intend to stay very quiet?"

"Who's in that barn?" a voice of authority demanded from just outside.

Bat flinched his shoulders and waved for Joshua to be still.

"Is jest me, Boss, Battis Johnston. Slave nigger."

"Where's Savannah?" Joshua whispered.

Bat didn't answer.

"Where?" Joshua repeated.

"Get out here nigger," the same voice said.

"Yessuh, right soon," Bat said, turning to go. He motioned for Joshua to stay down and hidden and put his hand over his mouth to instill silence.

"Now!"

"Yessuh, right now, I is coming."

Bat went outside. Joshua crawled quietly from the hay and crept to the side of the barn where he could look through the cracks in the boards. A dozen or more mounted cavalry sat their horses. On foot in front of them Joshua counted 4 ragged Union soldiers. Their hands were either tied with ropes or chained. They looked trampled and exhausted. Battis approached the riders, his ragged straw hat in his hands. He looked small standing in front of the horses. A major sat his horse in front of the others. He was lighting a cigar. The major's uniform looked worn and ragged and he looked thin. The horses viewed gaunt and tired. The troops behind lined up behind the major appeared rag-tag and weakened. Most were bearded with shoulder-length hair. All heavily armed with pistols, Carbines and sabers.

"Where's the boss man of this place, Nigger?" The major demanded.

"Well Suh," Bat said," da boss man, Master Johnston, is all off in ya'll's army. Him a colonel or sum'thin like dat."

"You the boss man now?"

"No Suh," Bat said, "Missy Savannah is da boss man... lady."

"Get her."

"Yes Suh, but she coming right now, she is."

Joshua could see Savannah approaching the riders. She looked thin and tired. Her face was drawn, worried. Her eyes dark, her auburn hair tied behind her head in a pony-tail and streaming down onto the middle of her back. One of the riders yelled when he saw her.

"Well hello Boss Man. Best look 'in boss man I ever seen."

The Major turned in his saddle, looked at the man that yelled.

"Shut your mouth, private."

A first sergeant turned in his saddle and pointed at the private and shook his head.

"Yes sir Major, but oh my, she is something."

The first sergeant spurred his horse over next to the private.

"Shut it, Gordon," he said quietly.

The private grinned at the sergeant. The sergeant shook his head ominously.

The major took a deep puff on his cigar and blew the smoke into the morning air.

"One more word, private."

"Yes sir," the private said, staring at Savannah.

The major tipped his hat to Savannah. She stood silently looking at the riders and then at the Union prisoners. She was small and frail in their presence; vulnerable. Joshua suddenly hated himself for being there. For putting Bat and Savannah in jeopardy. What would happen to them if these Rebel cavalry troops discovered they had been hiding him?

"Pardon Miss, but your name?" the major said.

"Savannah Johnston. This is Johnston Manor. My father is a colonel of infantry. I think he is fighting in the north. He's with the Stonewall Brigade."

"Yes Miss, I respect that, but we need food and blankets, we're gonna have to take what we need. Please don't cause trouble."

"We don't have much," Savannah said, "please leave us be. Colonel Johnston would want us left alone."

"Well I don't really care right now what Colonel Johnston wants," the major said, "we'll have to take what we need."

"I know what I need," a voice came from the back. Some of the other riders chuckled.

The major turned in his saddle again.

"I'll shoot the next man that opens his dirty mouth."

"Weren't me," the private said.

The major turned back to Savannah.

"I'm Major Morgan and know that the colonel will understand what we did here. He's likely doing the same thing up there in Virginia."

Savannah turned and walked toward the house.

"Then take what you need," she said, "...if you must."

"That an invite?" a voice came from the riders.

Major Morgan drew his revolver and turned toward his riders, then kicked his horse ahead and rode directly to the private. He sat quietly for a long moment staring at the trooper then suddenly swung his revolver hitting the private across the face and knocking him off his horse. He turned to the sergeant.

"Tend to him. And I'll shoot any man that touches that woman."

In less than two minutes the wounded private, his mouth and face bleeding, was sat back onto his horse. The riders were all silent.

"Anyone else here got a dirty mouth?" Major Morgan said.

"Seems Private Jamison oaught'a shut his," someone offered.

"It's shut now," the major said.

"Yes siree it is," someone said.

In the barn and watching all of this Joshua whispered, "Thank God for you Major." He felt a growing alarm for the safety of Savannah, knowing all too well the tendency of desperate soldiers to perpetrate the worse evils imaginable. For a moment he thought about giving himself up and saying he'd been hiding undiscovered in the barn. But felt that Major Morgan wouldn't believe him and would surely accuse Bat and Savannah of aiding the enemy and punish them.

Morgan ignored the comment and rode back to the head of the column.

Joshua was relieved to see Savannah go back to the house. He wished he had a pistol so he could try to defend Savannah and Battis. Again he silently thanked God that the major was in charge and taking no nonsense from his troops. He knew an act like shooting at these cavalry troops would cost him his life but he feared for Savannah and Battis.

"Just a minute Miss Johnston," the major said, "we're gonna have to shoot these here Yanks and I wanna know where you want them buried?"

Savannah stopped and turned around. She put her hands on her hips and suddenly looked resolute. Her dark brown eyes flared with anger.

"You aren't gonna shoot anyone on my property. If you want to act like animals then go into the woods…but not here."

Easy Savannah, Joshua thought. Don't push him.

"I'm afraid you don't have anything to say about it Miss Johnston. We'll bury them in that there field over yonder."

"No you won't," Savannah yelled, "that is where my momma and baby sister are buried. Don't you dare?"

"And...if we do?" a young lieutenant said, grinning, his hand on the butt of his pistol. Savannah scowled at him and shook her head.

Major Morgan turned to the lieutenant and raised his hand.

"After we take what we need," the major said," we're gonna execute these here criminals and we'll haul them into the trees over there and bury them. They'll be no more argument about it."

Savannah shook her head turned and went back to the house.

The major turned to Battis.

"Nigger, we need all your corn and meat. Don't hide even one morsel or I'll shoot you myself. And...find a shovel and pick. You're gonna dig a hole over yonder in them trees for these here yanks. One hole. One big hole."

The major turned to the lieutenant.

"Have the men strip these here prisoners and line them up agin the barn. Let's git on with this dirty business. Shape a firing squad. Least six men...better, eight."

"I'm gonna git me a Union coat," a voice came from the riders.

"Boots! I need dem boots," another rider yelled.

"You'll git what I give you," the major said.

Joshua crept back to a quiet, darkened place in the barn. He sat down, his face in his hands. His own soldiers, his brothers, were going to be shot in moments and he felt he had to do something. After all, he was a corporal in the Union Army and as far as he could tell these Yanks were all privates. It was his duty to take care of them. To do something. But he did nothing.

Fifteen minutes later he heard cavalrymen yelling at the prisoners to line up against the barn. He heard someone whimpering; another begging.

"Ya'll ain't really gonna shoot us are Major Sir?"

"Sure as God is mighty and Jeff Davis is President of these Confederate States," Joshua heard the major say.

Then he heard another pleading voice.

"Major Sir, how can ya be so mean?"

"God's will," Major Morgan said. "As I walk through the *Valley of Death* I fear no evil, except you bastards. I would kill a poisonous snake in the wink of an eye, yes I would, and I will for sure shoot you snakes. Make your peace with the almighty, that is if he'll be hearing it."

Another voice: "I can't stand here naked. That lady will see me."

"No for long," a voice said.

Joshua moved to a side of the barn where he could watch through the cracks. The four prisoners, all of them young, stood naked against the side of the barn. They shivered in unison and all held hands over their crotches. They were pale, skinny, tired and frail. They were unshaven and their hair hung long on their necks. One of the prisoners was weeping silently. Joshua could see tears running down his cheeks. One of the prisoners appeared to be the oldest, maybe 25 or 30. He was tall and large boned but thin, though he appeared strong and able. As he stood against the barn wall his continence was stern; almost rebellious. He stood glaring at the eight riflemen who had lined up twenty-five feet away and were waiting orders to shoot. The major stood off to the side of the firing squad with his saber drawn and held high against his right shoulder. The shooters stood at parade rest, their carbines butts grounded.

Suddenly the big soldier shrieked and charged the firing squad. He struck the first man square in the face with his fist sending him sprawling into the mud. The others dropped their rifles and began struggling with him. The major lowered his saber, took one quick step forward and plunged the glistening blade into the naked back of the struggling prisoner. The prisoner gasped, turned and struck out at the major. The major reacted by slashing the soldier across the face and then hacking down onto the top of his head. The soldier crumpled to his knees gasping for air. The lieutenant stepped up, drew his revolver and fired a pistol shot into the back of the soldier's head. He crumpled forward into the mud and lay still. Blood trickled out of his nose and mouth and one eye protruded out onto his cheek. The lieutenant nodded with a look of satisfaction on his face. The major nodded then wiped the blade of his saber on his trouser leg and resumed his execution stance. The riflemen recovered their rifles and fell back into formation. The stricken rifleman wiped his bloody nose and mouth on the sleeve of his coat. Two soldiers dragged the dead man out of the way like a meaningless sack of potatoes.

"Next?" the major said. "Anyone else like to challenge me?"

None of the prisoners moved or spoke. Joshua could smell the fear. Sickened, he moved away from the wall and staggered back to the hay mound and his blanket. As he sat down in the straw he heard the major shout and then heard a ripping volley of shots. Something rattled against the barn wall and Joshua could hear heavy thumps and groans as men fell. Then he heard the major say something about "finish the job." Several pistol shots sounded as someone administered the coup to the fallen prisoners.

"You, nigger," the major shouted, "git that hole dug and bury these men. Then report to me and give a hand to my troops rounding up forage."

Yes'suh Major sir," Joshua heard Bat say. "Right soon, Suh."

Then the major turned to the lieutenant.

"Lieutenant Brown, it is your job to keep the lady in the house and out of the way."

"Yes sir," the lieutenant said, grinning.

"And there is no harm to come to her. Is that understood?"

"Yes sir."

"And you have my permission to shoot any man that touches her. And I'll shoot you myself, likewise."

"Yes sir," the lieutenant said.

"Hell, it'd be worth it," a voice came from the troops.

The major turned and stared at the cavalrymen. To the man they each avoided eye-contact with the major.

CHAPTER SEVENTEEN

Battis

Hours later with the executed soldiers buried, those cavalrymen not occupied sat talking amongst themselves. There was considerable speculation as to what might the lieutenant be doing in the house with Miss Johnston. A foraging detail had been selected.

"C'mon nigger," Joshua heard a cavalryman yell. "Show me the good stuff in this here barn." Panicked, Joshua slipped into a darkened corner just as the sliding door opened. Bat and a tall trooper entered into the gloom. The trooper held a revolver in his right hand.

"Ain't too all much in da barn, Suh," Bat said. "Most of da good stuff has gone away to da war with Colonel Johnston and his regiment."

"Ya'll got horses and we need them," the trooper said.

"We's on'y got two and I's really need'im fo da work in da field."

"Git them out," the trooper said," and any tack that goes with-it."

"Yes Suh, but I's wish 'in ya wouldn't."

"Ya'll can wish your ass off, Nigger, but it won't help."

"If it has to be dat way," Bat said.

As Bat and the trooper walked toward the stalls the soldier suddenly drew up short and pointed at Joshua's blanket and the remains of some food laying in the hay. He turned quickly and aimed the revolver at Bat's head.

"What's this?" he yelled.

Bat looked frightened and began shaking his head.

"I's mostly live in da barn, Missy don't like niggers too much."

The trooper waved the pistol in Bat's face.

"Don't' lie to me nigger. I'll shoot your black ass off."

The trooper cocked the revolver and shoved against Bat's chest.

"No Suh, I's ain't lying, Suh. Missy Johnston don't like niggers one bit."

"Hell you ain't, nigger. I'll git the major in here and you quit lying."

Joshua took a deep breath and stepped out of the gloom. The trooper swung the revolver toward him.

"Who the...?" he yelled.

"Hired hand," Joshua said quietly.

"Fuck you are," the trooper said. "Ya'll a God damned Yank. That's north talk if 'in I ever heard it."

"Confederate sympathizer," Joshua said.

"The hell you are," the trooper said. "I'll shoot your ass off right now."

He aimed the pistol at Joshua.

Bat swung one of his huge fists and struck the trooper behind the right ear. He toppled into the hay as if he'd been shot. Then he rolled onto his back, grasping in the hay for the fallen revolver. Bat dropped with his knees onto the chest of the trooper and grabbed his throat in both hands. Joshua rushed toward them and retrieved the revolver from the hay. Bat held the pressure on the trooper's throat until he quit struggling, there was a final short gurgle, and then silence.

"I kilt him," Bat whispered. "Oh sweet lordy, I kilt him."

"Kingsley," a voice yelled from outside the barn, "what's go 'in on in there?"

Joshua stepped back into the gloom and aimed the revolver toward the door. He heard footsteps approach. Bat stood up and put his hand out for the revolver. Joshua looked at the gun and then handed it to Bat. Bat dropped it beside the dead man. Dark figures entered the doorway.

"What the hell…?" someone yelled.

The men crouched at the body.

"Mother of God," one said, "this nigger killed Kingsley."

He looked up at Bat.

Bat raised his hands into the air. Joshua stayed back out of sight in the deep gloom. He watched in disgust and with a growing nausea in his stomach as the two soldiers pointed their pistols at Bat and marched him outside. Joshua stood there hating himself. He'd stood by and let that faithful black man cover for him and protect him without a word of protest. Going out the barn door Bat looked back over his shoulder. One of the troopers jabbed his revolver into Bat's side.

"Major, major Morgan," one yelled.

"Major, this nigger killed Kingsley," another yelled.

"What the hell for?" a voice said.

"Because he's a violent nigger," another voice said.

"Search him," another voice said. "He probably robbed Kingsley.

"Yeah, we caught the son-of-a-bitch red-handed."

"We'll hang him," a voice came back.

Joshua watched in silence while the major and the first sergeant came into the barn and examined the body. With the pistol, he thought, I could have killed them both. The major and the sergeant left and then two troopers came into the barn and carried the dead man out. Then he heard the major shouting at Battis.

"Dig another hole nigger and you can bury this here soldier ya'll kilt. Then dig another hole for yourself somewhere out there in woods. We ain't burying any niggers near this soldier, not even near the yanks."

"Your soder was beat 'in on me Major sir and I's ony protect 'in myself," Bat pleaded.

"Makes no difference to me," the major said. You're a dead man."

Through the slats in the barn wall Joshua watched as they tied Bat to a tree in the front yard. A soldier was assigned to guard him.

"Why'nt we just shoot him right now?" a voice said.

"Too good for him. Shoot 'in is the way soldiers die. We'll hang him in the morning. Let him suffer some during the night. Looks like rain. See that he gets nothing, not even a drink of water. And strip him."

Joshua spent a sleepless night without food or any contact from Savannah. It was increasingly cold and damp in the barn and before morning it began to rain. He worried constantly about Savannah knowing that several of the cavalry troops were sleeping in the house. He felt sick about Bat and searched his mind trying to form a plan where he and Bat could escape before the hanging. He knew that what had happened to Bat was his fault. He should never have stopped at Johnston Manor. Should never had stayed in their barn and should never have asked for, or expected Battis to help. Worse than that if the major found out that Savannah had been hiding a Union Soldier she may also be hung or at the least imprisoned. Joshua decided to leave before dawn. Half an hour later he changed his mind. He wouldn't leave until he knew Savannah was safe.

He would risk his neck by hiding in the barn and exposing himself only if it became necessary to interfere with the troops and protect Savannah. Battis Johnston was to be hung at dawn for the murder of Private Robert Kingsley. Joshua had heard Bat vocally refuse to dig his own grave or that of the dead trooper. A voice of one of the troops had responded by saying that they'd "feed him to the hogs…if they'll have that nigger meat."

The night was as black and interminable as a pit. Joshua could not sleep. He went often to the door and peered out into the dark trying to see Battis. There was nothing other than the occasional glow of a guard's cigar or pipe. Infrequently he heard the guard say something to Battis but there was never the sound of a reply. Regularly every two hours the guard was relieved by another and there was always some muted conversation between them. Joshua could guess that Savannah was awake in the house and likely saying prayers for God's protection of Battis.

As the sky lightened in the east Joshua heard Battis praying quietly. The resonance brought tears to his eyes:
> "Oh Lordy, my Father up there in heaven,
> why, like your boy say long tam ago, has
> you forsaken me. If'n you have to take me
> today please forgive me those sins of mine
> and forgive me for let' in my chile pass to you
> when maybe I's could'a dun sum'thin mo.
> I's hoping ya'll will take me to ya'll's arms on this
> last day oh mine and please my dear Lordy love
> and protect Missy Savannah fo all tams. Pray
> please ya'll bring her daddy back safe from da
> war…and soon. My Missy need her daddy very
> much and please take good care of Corporal

Cole and let him survive this war…too…and come on back here to Missy. I knows they so much in love. No sir, these young ones cain't fool an ole nigger man…theys in love. Amen."

Half an hour later Joshua's heart broke when he heard Savannah crying and pleading with the major to spare Battis life. He heard her say something about having been with Battis since she'd been a child. Then he'd heard a trooper's voice say something like, "Betch'cha been with that nigger other ways too. Lordy, he's hung like a mule."

"Shut your dirty mouth," Major Gordon yelled.

Joshua was watching through the cracks in the wood. Battis had been stripped naked, his hands tied behind his back. He'd refused a blindfold. He was standing quietly beneath a large oak tree in the front yard, a hemp rope with a hangman's noose thrown over a limb. He watched as Savannah approached him in the rain. She looked frail and panicky. She knew there was no time left. Joshua felt hate for himself. He had caused all this sadness. He had changed Savannah's life forever. He heard her whisper softly to him. Would she hate him now? Would she turn away from him? Ask him to leave before he caused more pain?

"Oh Missy Savannah please go' wan away. I's not decent for ya'll to be see' in me."

He heard Savannah whisper again. He could see tears streaming down her cheeks and he recognized that she hadn't slept during the night.

"Oh no Missy Savannah you go' wan in da house. I's doan want ya'll to see this. God bless you Missy. You knows I's loved you since you was borned. You's like my very own child. I's loves you jus like I loves my little girl gone lang time now to Heaven."

Joshua moved away from the wall sat down in the hay and wept.

"What have I done?" he said aloud.

The barn-yard grew quiet. Joshua heard the house door close sharply. He knew Savannah had gone inside. Then a low cheer of sorts erupted, followed by a pistol shot. Then someone yelled, "Cut him down." An hour later Joshua heard the cavalrymen mount up and ride silently out of the yard. A gloomy quiet settled over Johnston Plantation. Much later, after not hearing anything from Savannah, Joshua left the barn and walked to the house. He found Savannah crying in her bedroom. He sat on the edge of the bed and took her hand in his. She sat up and put her arms around him.

"Savannah, I am so sorry. This is all my fault. I'll go away, but I know I've damaged you forever. I shouldn't have come here…I know that."

Savannah drew back and looked at him.

"It isn't you or me or those soldiers," she said, "it's this awful war."

Joshua spent the rest of the day with Savannah. In time she stopped crying and became rather resolute. They discussed burying Bat and pondered what her future would be on the plantation without him. She also knew that Joshua planned to leave and go back north in search of his regiment. She knew he didn't want to be considered a deserter and wanted to do his duty as a Union soldier. Joshua recognized that leaving Savannah alone in this war-torn land was a precarious prospect. The thought that maybe she could go north with him quickly escaped his mind. That evening, after caring for Bat's body, they fixed a meager meal and spent the evening in front of a fire. That night Joshua slept alone in front of the fireplace.

It was raining lightly the following morning as Joshua clambered out of the hole he had dug for Bat's grave and tossed the pick and shovel aside. He stretched his aching back and arms and looked at Savannah. She was standing under a nearby Oak tree with a shawl wrapped around her shoulders. Her auburn hair was damp from the rain and wet curls clung to her forehead. Joshua could see her shivering. She had been crying earlier but now stood quietly making an valiant attempt toward stoicism. Joshua moved around the grave to Savannah and put his arm around her shoulder.

"You're shivering," he said. "You gonna be alright?"

Savannah leaned against him and rested her head on his shoulder.

"I'm frightened," she whispered.

"Don't be frightened," Joshua said. "Things will be alright."

"No they won't." She turned her head upward and looked into his eyes.

"Why?" Joshua said.

"It's the rain and all this."

"What about the rain?" Joshua said.

"I'm afraid of it."

"Why are you afraid of the rain?"

"No reason."

"There must be a reason?" Joshua said.

"No," Savannah said.

"Can't you tell me?"

Savannah was quiet for a long moment then looked away toward a distant tree line.

"Because…I see myself dead in the rain."

Later they'd lowered Bat's body into his grave. Joshua had spent some of the previous afternoon nailing together a rough pine coffin. The pine wood was so green that it still dripped sap and the sap ran down the sides of the coffin in tiny rivulets. That night Joshua could still smell the aroma of the sap on his hands and clothes. They'd wrapped Bat in wool blankets, laid him on his back and crossed his hands. Savannah had put Bat's pipe and tobacco bag in the coffin along with his old straw hat and bible. They'd stood at the edge of the grave after it was filled in while Joshua read some passages from the Johnston family bible. The grave marker had been fashioned from a broad piece of oak wood with Bat's name and date of death carved into the surface. Savannah had fashioned a bouquet of flowers picked in the meadow for the grave. Savannah stood quietly for a while at the foot of the grave and then began to softly sing...

"Oh Shenandoah, I long to see you,
far away, you rolling river.
Oh Shenandoah, I'm bound to leave you,
Away you rolling river...'tis seven years
I've been a rover...away...you rolling river..."

Then it rained hard all afternoon and all night.

CHAPTER EIGHTEEN

The Days

The days with Savannah at Johnston Manor became magical for Joshua; the nights even more so. He and Savannah began spending all their time together. Joshua took over the many chores that had belonged to Bat. In the evenings they prepared a meal with whatever could be found, lit candles, sat together eating and conversing about their many myriad interests.

Joshua was surprised to learn that Savannah painted in oils when she could get them, and much to the chagrin of her father, had been an art major at college with a paternally coalesced side in agriculture. After a few days and gaining Joshua's artistic trust she took him to a storage room where her paintings were kept.

Joshua was startled at the quality of her work and even those paintings he did not understand or even recognize the contents or the forms. Savannah had quietly explained a new art philosophy she had learned at school in Pennsylvania. A few of the professors were teaching a new idea that a painting could simply be interesting forms, shapes, and colors and that a painting did not necessarily have to be 'something' and that it did not have to represent or be representative. They had explained that art was in the mind of the beholder and could even be an image from the dark, or enlightened recesses of his or her mind and they also taught that women painters were now accepted and coming into their own with great and outstanding works. A woman's name they mentioned was Berthe Morisot. Savannah thought that she wanted emulate Miss Morisot.

Her professors had introduced her to a new avant-garde movement in Europe being called Impressionism. Impressionism was the start for some artists in Europe allowing themselves to think away from the traditionalism of the great masters and to begin creating a new art form that did not require established colors, shapes, or subjects. They were allowing themselves to experiment with new colors, hews, shapes, forms, sunlight, shadows and subjects. Impressionism was expanding the world of art like no other innovation had throughout the centuries. The Impressionist had allowed themselves to create works of art in form and design rather than scenery, people, buildings, or animals, and especially the centuries old religious compositions. The professors were tossing about the names of artists in Europe who were experimenting with Impressionism: Camille Pissarro, Claude Monet, August Renoir, Edgar Degas, and a host of others. Joshua discovered that he liked the idea of this new movement called Impressionism.

Joshua, gaining the needed confidence after hearing Savannah nervously expose her passion for art and painting, told her his desire was to write and create great works in literature, and even poetry. Very much enthused and encouraged by Joshua's revelation Savannah asked him to compose a poem for her on the spot. Joshua protested but then coalesced when she first begged and then looked disappointed. When he agreed she disappeared for a few minutes returning

with ink, quill and paper. Joshua took a deep breath and went
to work:

> He came out of the night,
> Standing straight and strong,
> Unafraid to guard the gate.
> A dark devil or bright saint?
> He floated into the gloom
> And brought the morning light.
> Bracing the worn upon high,
> He looked down upon the weary
> Lifted him up and shook his mane
> To smile and sigh and keep,
> This dark apparition of a restive sleep.

Savannah reached over, took the paper, read it silently and
then aloud. Joshua thought he could see moisture in her eyes
and reached and took her hand.

"It is about Bat, isn't it? She said quietly.

"Yes," Joshua said.

"I'll keep it forever," Savannah said.

Joshua and Savannah were sitting on the wide veranda
that encircled the Johnston Manor House. The sun was sitting
through fading rain clouds and the air was fresh and clean
and they could smell the wet trees in the yard. It was cool so
Savannah had a shawl wrapped around her shoulders and
another over her legs. Joshua wore one of Bat's old jackets
loosely over his shoulders.

"The rain is gone for a while, Savannah said. "…I hope
anyway."

"Let's go inside and light a fire," Joshua said, "you're cold."

"The rain always chills me," Savannah said.

"I know. Move closer. I'll keep you warm, Savannah?"

"Yes."

"There is no place in the World I would rather be than right here with you."

Savannah looked up at Joshua and smiled.

"Not even with Katie Hespeth?" she said.

"I don't know any Katie," Joshua said, looking away.

"Oh you remember," Savannah said, "that Belle of the Ball back there in Hanover?"

"Nope! And just be quiet about what's-her-name."

"Oh you'll meet another girl soon as you go back North and forget me over-night," Savannah said.

"Won't neither," Joshua said. "Fact is I'll love you 'til I die."

They were sitting on a wide swing, the one Bat had put up for Savannah just a few weeks before he died. Savannah moved against Joshua and he put his arm around her. Then she turned and faced him on the seat putting her chest against his and her arms around his neck. Joshua put his arms around her and squeezed her tightly against him.

"Don't break me, silly boy," Savannah said.

Joshua kissed her hair. "I'd like to squeeze your heart right into mine,"

"I think you're going to," Savannah said. Then she reached up and kissed him on the neck.

Beyond the barn and the outbuildings Joshua could see Bat's grave. The mound of dirt was wet and the marker was leaning to one side and he could see the wilted flowers Savannah had placed there. He knew it was his fault that Bat was dead. His fault because he had come to Johnston Manor. He'd had no right to stop there. He'd had no right to expect help or accept help from southerners.

After all he was a yank and his army was invading the South. Hadn't Union General William Tecumseh Sherman said something about making the Southerners howl? Joshua knew now that he had done his part in making the people he'd learned to love, howl. He lamented it, but he was so much in love with Savannah Johnston that he couldn't bring himself to regret the past few days, or his decision on that lonely rainy night to stop at the plantation looking for anything that might ease his suffering.

"You're thinking," Savannah said.

Joshua squeezed her tightly. "Hmmm, about us."

Savannah kissed his neck. "...And what about us?"

"Our future together," he said.

"We don't have a future together," Savannah said.

"What?" Joshua said.

Savannah rested her cheek against his chest.

"You'll go away forever. I know you will."

"I won't."

"You will, "Savannah said softly, "I feel it."

"I can't become a deserter from the army," Joshua said, "but I can go back and fix it. If I desert they'll shoot me. They do that you know."

"But you won't come back to me. Will you think of me now and then?"

"I will," Joshua said. "but I won't have to. I'll be right here with you."

"How much longer do we have?" Savannah said.

Joshua squeezed her against him. "A day or two."

"No," Savannah said, "a week or two. Please."

"Let's go in," Joshua said.

Savannah took Joshua by the hand and led him into the house.

"Let's sleep on the floor in front of the fire," Savannah said.

"We'll make a bed right here," Joshua said.

"Yes, we'll sleep here together. You can keep me warm…for now."

"I'll keep you warm forever," Joshua said.

Three days later Savannah found Joshua wrapping his effects into an oil cloth. She stood very still, watching him. He tried to avoid her eyes.

"Do you have to?" Savannah said. "Why today? Why not tomorrow?"

Joshua moved over to Savannah and put his arms around her. She stood very still, looking up at him. Her eyes were beginning to tear.

"Yes," he said. "I need to take that first dreadful step."

"Today?" Savannah said.

"Yes," Joshua said, not looking at her. "But I don't want to."

Savannah turned and walked out of the house onto the veranda and sat down on the swing. Joshua came out onto the porch and sat beside her and took her hand in his. Then he kissed her hand. He saw that she was crying.

"First Bat, and now you," she said. "I'm losing the people I love. I just can't be alone here. What will I do? There will be no point in anything."

"Walk a ways with me, "Joshua said.

Savannah walked with Joshua along a road that led from Johnston Manor into the forest. They stopped on a wooden bridge that crossed a small stream. Joshua turned and leaned back against the bridge railing. He could hear the gurgle of water rushing beneath the bridge, it was a lonely sound. He wanted to close his ears to it. Savannah leaned on the opposite rail and stood quietly looking down into the water. Joshua spoke to her quietly.

"Missy Savannah…look at me."

Savannah didn't turn.

"Don't call me that," she said, "it reminds me of Battis. It was always Missy Savannah with him."

"I know you miss him. I'm sorry."

"He was more of a father to me than my father. Yes, a black man. He taught me to fish in this very stream when I was six years old. He taught me to ride horses, things he was always too busy to do, and he taught me about his people, the ones brought over from Africa and sold like cattle. He told me about how hundreds died in the holds of those horrible ships and how their bodies were simply tossed over the side. Josh, I know we've been wrong here in the South. You know Bat didn't hate white folks, he should have, but couldn't hate, it wasn't in his soul. He died for you, Josh, and for me. Now go, if you must."

Savannah turned away not looking at Joshua and walked slowly back along the dirt road to the house. He could hear her crying.

"Savannah," Joshua called out.

Savannah did not look back or answer. He watched her until she was out of sight, then turned and began walking north. He would return to Savannah, he knew he would.

It looked like rain.

CHAPTER NINETEEN

Walking North

By sunset of the third day away from Savannah Joshua had eaten all the food she had given him and he began searching out farms and plantations along the way and stealing from barns and corn-cribs. Savannah had given him matches dipped in hot wax to protect them from the rain and damp, and one of Bat's old copper boiling kettles saying that she knew Bat would want him to have it. With the kettle he was able to boil and eat whatever forage he had found along the way. A good day of foraging was one when he found a vegetable or a piece of fruit. At days end everything went into the pot and when boiled provided some form of eatable stew. A combination of apple, carrot, corn and sometimes greens provided a welcome meal at sundown even if it was never enough. But his twilight dinners, if you could call them dinners, were a lonely affair with the memory of his days and nights with Savannah Johnston, pushing him to the borders of sorrow. He'd developed the habit of burying his face in her blankets at night in order to doze with her scent easing his loneliness and feelings of desperation. Daily he fought the burning desire to turn back south and return to Johnston Manor and the woman he had fallen very much in love with. He felt that he would go crazy if he thought too much about Savannah.

Joshua tried without success to overcome the persistent feeling that he had abandoned Savannah to an unknown fate and increasing danger. A woman alone in that war torn countryside was vulnerable to marauding soldiers, guerrillas, or even starving locals. Strong and self-assured Savannah Johnston had reluctantly urged him to follow his conscience and return to his army and finish what he had started so long ago in Pennsylvania, but behind is back she had wept knowing that he was leaving her and that in all probability their life together was at an end. Without Battis and the former few slaves at Johnston Manor she was totally alone and must rely on her own wits and strength to survive until her father could return home from the war. That is, if he survived. Joshua had known of her thinking and anxiety about the possibility that Hector Johnston would not endure the war. He knew that at times she had gone alone to stand on the little wooden bridge near the manor looking wistfully north hoping, beyond hope, that she would see her father riding home with his obligation to the Southern Rebellion complete. There was no way she could have known that she would never see him again.

In the meantime the war was going quite well for the armies of the North. General Ulysses S. Grant was now general of the armies. Abraham Lincoln had settled on him for a leader after he displayed great tactical knowledge and fearlessness as a commander. The great and decisive three day battle at Gettysburg was history. Robert E. Lee had taken a disastrous beating on a hill called Little Round Top and on a ridge name Culp's Hill. He had taken his trampled army quickly back across the Potomac River leaving thousands of his dead and wounded on the field. From that point on Lee was forced to fight defensively in almost every encounter with the Union Army. At the beginning of the war Lee, a Union general at the time, had been offered leadership of all northern troops but being a Virginian by birth, had chosen to 'go south' and eventually became the commander of all southern troops. Lee had lost Stonewall Jackson at Chancellorsville, probably his greatest commander and tactician. Jackson, like Union General William Tecumseh Sherman, was a offensive fighter and chose always to carry the fight to the enemy. The Union leadership at that time knew, without a doubt, that Jackson's untimely death was a blessing to the Union Cause. Whereas the Confederate Army's General James Longstreet was a defensive fighter and chose to defend territory. But now without Jackson, Longstreet became the South's preeminent leader and was soon nicknamed by Lee, *My Old War Horse.*

Laying wrapped in Savannah's blankets he recounted, over and over, how they had first decided they were in love. It had begun with an unruly impulse as she had brought his dinner to the barn. He looked up stammered, then abruptly blurted out, "Savannah, you are beautiful, you really are." Savannah had blushed, shook her head in disagreement and left the barn without speaking. Joshua had hated himself for his brash outburst. Would he have to leave now? Would she be afraid of him? Would she think ill of him? Think he was an ungrateful clod? A classic impetuous Yank?

That however had been Joshua's last day in the barn. An hour later Savannah had come back, taken him by the hand and without a word led him to the kitchen where she'd prepared a simple dinner. A dusty bottle of imported French wine had been found in what was left of Hector Johnston's wine cellar and they'd celebrated their first real meal together.

Later that evening as they lazed in front of a roaring fireplace Joshua had suddenly leaned down close to Savannah as she lay on her back propped on several pillows half-dozing and dressed comfortably in one of her father's long dress shirts and riding pants. Now he remembered it as *the night of the rules* and everything as it had happened.

"I have a dire suspicion about you," he'd said.

"Well?" Savannah had said, watching him closely.

"You hold still while I check this out," Joshua said.

Then he slowly raised the bottom of her shirt until he could see her bare midriff. Savannah watched unmoving, but smiling.

"Yes?" she said.

Joshua looked up from her midriff and beamed.

"Just as I thought," he said, "you have a belly-button."

Savannah giggled and cuffed him on the shoulder.

"Of course I do silly boy, everyone does."

"Not as pretty as yours," Joshua said.

"How would you know?" Savannah said. "How many girls' belly-buttons have you inspected?"

"Oh dozens," Joshua said, "I'm an expert."

Savannah cuffed him again, shaking her head.

"Silly boy."

Joshua reached over and cautiously took her right hand in his.

"Yours is the only one," he said. Then he kissed the back of her hand, turned it over and kissed the palm. Savannah watched, unmoving. Now Joshua laid his cheek against Savannah's belly and looking into her eyes, turned and kissed her stomach. Savannah drew in a quick breath. "Oh, oh," she whispered, "that's against the rules."

"This isn't controlled by rules. There are no rules in love," Joshua said.

Then he moved up and kissed her forehead.

"Joshua David Cole," Savannah said, "control yourself. Your breaking all the rules."

Now he gently kissed her hair and then both high-boned cheeks and then her neck.

"Corporal Cole," Savannah whispered, "what are you doing?"

Joshua moved a little and lightly kissed her lips, then pulled back and gazed into her eyes. She rose up and kissed him. Joshua took her face in his hands, held her, and kissed her again, lingering for long moments.

"I love you Missy Savannah and there ain't nothing you can do about it."

"I love you too Joshua Cole. And don't say ain't."

Later that night they broke another rule.

And now as he lay alone, he decided he did not love the ground with its wet smell of dead leaves, grass, and tree bark. His stomach ached. He needed to eat. For God's sake, yes, he needed to eat, drink, and be with Savannah. Yes, beautiful Savannah with the hair he would never want her to change… and now he lay achingly remembering how he had loved to watch her comb and brush her hair.

CHAPTER TWENTY

Sweet Chariot

On the sixth day after Leaving Johnston Manor Joshua came to a river that was swollen by two days of heavy off and on rain. He was wet and chilled. He hadn't eaten anything for a day and a half. The momentary comfort of his nightly hot tea had drawn to a close. The tea leaves Savannah had given him were gone. He'd kept the leaves and used them over and over until they were depleted of any semblance of flavor and then dumped them into his infrequent pots of boiled forage for the added nourishment, if any.

On this lifeless morning the river seemed to speak to him, warning that it was a *river of no return*, now stemming his progress north and threatening to strip him of what few things he carried. Joshua had been a strong swimmer since early childhood but the swollen current and his present state of limitation predicted a certain doom in his thoughts and lagging determination. But at the same time he couldn't help but think that perhaps he was overreacting to the river and that his present lack of self-confidence was causing too much caution and he had to considered the reality that just a brief year or two past he wouldn't have hesitated to plunge into a current such as this one, and recognizing the thought that this very river, in its bloated state, would have likely challenged his personal idea of manhood.

On his march north Joshua had been keeping the afternoon sun to his left, that is when there had been any sun, and at all times yearning for the warmth it would offer and the heat that would dry his clothing and blankets. But that kindness had remained unseen hiding above sinister clouds that dampened his clothing and his spirits more often than not on a daily basis. Now as the day faded and the lonely evening crept in Joshua sat by his small fire listening to the growl of the river, not unlike the growl of his stomach. His tiny fire offered little help in his effort to get warm and dry. He gazed off into the night and said aloud, "Not far my little fire throws its beam." His own voice in the gloom startled him. He sat with the oil cloth wrapped around his shoulders while looking toward the west and watching the remains of a frail sunset as it slipped carelessly beneath the darkening clouds on its way to brighten someone's new day.

Short minutes later dark closed in and Joshua's minute fire seemed to brighten the frail arc of light his camp occupied but failed to lift his spirits. Too often in the mystifying murmur of the river he felt he could hear Savannah calling to him. He decided that the river had an accent of its own and callously enjoyed tormenting him with the familiar echo of voices he had known and loved. When the torture grew too painful he rolled up in his Savannah scented blankets attempting to find a sleep that might shut out those troubling voice-like incursions. As he dozed sporadically throughout the night the memories of those spare but wonderful meals with Savannah lingered, niggling in and out of his slumber like a phantom that would not die away. He tossed wildly, feeling that strange unease in his legs and body that would not let him rest. At times during the darkest hour he felt virtually ill with his longing for Savannah Johnston and what had been. He now thought of his days with her as the most significant element of his life while his boyhood farm and his war experiences slowly faded to shadow and then to dark.

At dawn Joshua shook off the bitter chains of night and pushed back Savannah's blankets. He looked toward the dead embers of the evenings fire pit and Bat's pot hanging alone and empty. He gathered up the blankets, oil cloth and pot and tied them into a single bundle. In dread he sat down cross-legged on the river bank staring across and trying to envision himself on the other side, safe and wet but still in possession of his effects. Sitting there he verbally damned his weakness from lack of food and shelter and the arduous journey north. Once again he turned and looked toward the south knowing that somewhere out there beneath that dreary morning sky Savannah Johnston was alone without love or joy. He sat there struggling once more with the all but over-powering longing to turn south and walk back to her.

As he sat staring at the threatening deluge the recollections of those nights at Johnston Manor with Savannah lingered, sneaking in and out of his conscience like a annoying spirit that would just not leave him in peace.

That treasured night of *breaking the rules* weighed heavily on his mind and his regret that another of those loving *nights by the fire* may never become a certainty. He knew now that his love for Katie Hespeth had vanished as quickly as the whisper of Savannah's hair against his cheek. Back with his regiment he would write to Katie and try to explain.

Shaking his head he managed to break his trance, and then clambered unsteadily to his feet, shouldered his bedroll and turned to face the rain inflated river. Watching the river through the ghostly mists of dawn he recalled those childhood dreams where he'd needed to run but couldn't, his feet stuck to the earth. Now the river seemed to symbolized all those childhood night-time fears of dungeons and dragons and his feeble escape attempts from nameless monsters and unknown forest ogres.

Just then he heard the singing. It appeared to roll down the river on the surface of the water. The source of the singing was out of sight but seemed just up the river echoing hauntingly around the bend. "Swing low, sweet chariot, a coming for to carry me home.

Swing low sweet chariot..."

First it appeared as an apparition. Silently the ghost-like object seemed to hide in a grey mist rising from the water and then it became clearer and then took shape and became a flat-bottom boat. The singing had stopped abruptly. There were people on the boat, dark figures huddled together with a larger figure at the stern steering with a long pole-like oar. As the boat came closer it took on a greater shape and appeared to have been constructed of rough-hewn logs tied together by lengths of hemp rope. A crudely constructed sail topped a cross-bar rig near the center of the craft. The canvas or blanket sail was furled and secured near the bottom of the cross-member. Joshua smiled. The mast resembled the

Cross of the Crucifixion. This leaning toward Christianity was not uncommon amongst the black sufferers of slavery. Joshua guessed rightfully that the passengers on the boat where a slave family or others escaping indenture in the south. What was it Savannah had said, something about Abe Lincoln's Emancipation Proclamation freeing the slaves?

As the boat drew nearer Joshua could see the people on board talking amongst themselves and pointing in his direction. He waved. He felt no fear of negroes. The tall man at the stern cautiously waved back. The others sat silently now and looking furtively toward the tall man. The raft swung toward shore and Joshua got up and walked to the edge of the water. As the raft touched the shoreline the tall man tossed a length of hemp rope to Joshua and he pulled the raft as far onto the sand and gravel as he could.

The huddled women and children remained silent and staring. The big black man stepped off the raft and walked slowly to Joshua. He seemed to be studying Joshua's clothing. Then his eyes raised and met Joshua's.

"You a Union soder?"

Joshua hesitated, studying the expression on the man's face. His face remained composed, demonstrating neither serenity nor fear. They stood facing each other. Then the man smiled and reached out his hand. Joshua nodded and took the hand, it was calloused, thick, and powerful.

"Corporal Joshua Cole," Joshua said quietly, "Army of the United States."

The big man turned to the people on the raft. "It is alright Mama. This gentleman is a soder of the United States."

Joshua gave a small wave and smiled at the people still huddled on the raft. The older black woman smiled back and reached over and gave the younger woman a slight cuff on the shoulder.

"Mavis honey say hello to the soder."

The young woman still appeared unsure but forced a slight smile and nodded at Joshua. Three young children smiled and waved in unison.

"This here is my fambly, Mister Cole. That there is my Momma, Isabella, and my wife Mavis. Those three little ones is my children."

"And you?" Joshua asked.

"Moses."

"Happy to meet you and your family, Moses. Where ya'll heading?"

Moses hesitated. "Where's ya'll head 'in Mister Cole?"

Joshua smiled. Moses was being careful.

"North," Joshua said, "to rejoin my army. I was captured and sent to a Confederate prison further south. I escaped and been walking north for several days."

Moses smiled. "You ain't a deserter from the army?"

"No Moses, I ain't a deserter."

Moses appeared to relax. He turned to the people on the raft and told them to get off and brings some food. The children jumped off and began running about, laughing and shoving each other. The two women gathered large bundles of possessions and walked past Joshua being careful not to get too close. The younger woman looked at him with just a hint of fear in her eyes as if she expected him to suddenly spring at her. Moses reached out took her arm and stopped her.

"Mavis honey, this here soder is on our side. He's come here to free us black folks from the abuse in the south."

Mavis remained silent, avoiding Joshua's eyes. Joshua observed that her color was light, perhaps the influence of whites in her past, and he became aware of how attractive she was. It made him think of white plantation masters that seduced or even raped black women. He remembered what Bat had told him about the white foreman on the Johnston Plantation. It seemed that white plantation masters owned more than just the labor of their slaves. They owned their bodies too and the slaves had no say and no choice in how they were used or abused.

Joshua reached out his hand to Mavis. She ignored him, turned and walked away toward Isabella and the children.

"I'm sorry Mister Cole," Moses said, "my wife was abused by Confederate soldiers a few weeks ago and she is still terrified of uniforms."

Joshua looked down at the remaining rags of his uniform.

"I understand," Joshua said, "she doesn't have to apologize to me or anyone else." Then Joshua was reminded that Savannah was alone now.

"Mavis honey," Moses said, "set up some vittles for us and we'll eat. Mister Cole here looks like he ain't et regular for weeks."

Joshua raised both hands. "Moses, ya'll don't have to provide for me. You've got a lot of mouths to feed. I'll just be on my way. I've got to git across this river somehow so I can continue my walk north."

Moses turned and looked at the river. "She's kind of swollen right now, ain't she? Her names the Oconee River and she be 'in a bad girl.'"

"The rains," Joshua said. "Wrong time of year for me to be crossing rivers."

Moses looked back and smiled. "Well Mister Cole we'll eat and then I'll take you across the river. Of course ya'll is welcome to go on with us."

"Moses, you don't owe me anything. It's better you go on your way. I don't want you to put your family in anymore danger than you have to."

"Let me just say I's do'in my part for Abrim Limcoln and his army."

"I can't thank you too much," Joshua said. "Where are you and your family going?"

"We's go'in north to the Promised Land. Up there where folks don't hate Black folks the way southern folks do."

Joshua thought about Savannah and Bat.

"They all don't hate you folks," he said.

"Been so in my life," Moses said.

Mavis and Isabella laid a cake of corn bread and a pot of dark baked beans on the wooden box Moses had carried ashore and set out several cracked and broken plates and cups. Moses and his family sat on rags of blankets on the ground and invited Joshua to join them. They sat eating quietly and drinking cider poured from a crockery jar into crockery cups. Mavis admonished the children to quit staring at the Union 'soder.' They weren't listening and the little girl even summoned enough courage to reach out and touch Joshua's arm. Moses admonished her warning that "It ain't polite to touch folks unbidden."

"That is quite alright," Joshua said to Moses, "she's a lovely child and just curious as she ought to be. I must be a strange sight for her."

Then he smiled at her and reached out and patted her hand. Mavis scowled at Joshua and shook her head.

"You ain't sleep' in, Mister Cole," Mavis said.

"Mavis!" Isabella warned her daughter-in-law.

Joshua broke the mood. "What work did they have you doing on the plantation, Moses?"

"Mostly farm' in," Moses said, "but I'm also a very good black-smith and likes to work with iron. Farm' in tools is my specialty but I's make knives like you ain't seen before."

Before he shoved the raft back into the current, Joshua spoke to Mavis.

"Miss, I am so sorry about what happened to you. This terrible war has hurt many people, but you still have your life and your family. I hope you can go on and have a good life in the north. You must take what is left and make the most of it.

I've had to leave the woman I love alone here in this dangerous land. I pray for her every day and night and I will, God willing, return to her. That is what I am trying to do with my life. God bless you and Moses and your mother and these children."

Mavis just sat very still on the boat and looked away up the river while Joshua spoke. She didn't acknowledge him. Then they were gone.

CHAPTER TWENTY-ONE

Abel Witherspoon

As Moses and his family drifted north and around a bend in the river Joshua heard them resume their singing:

'Swing low, sweet chariot,
a coming for
to carry me home...'

He stood staring at the bend in the river and thinking about the simple kindness this family had shown him with no real reason to help. No real reason to share their meager supply of food. And no real reason to risk their safety further by foraging him across the river. In his bedroll was a huge cake of cornbread and a pound or so of cured ham, food he knew they needed but insisted he take. When he could no longer hear them singing he looked up at the mid-morning sky and thought he saw a suggestion of sunshine peeking through sinister clouds. He felt that Moses and his family and that hint of sunshine was a good omen. With renewed hope he shouldered his bedroll and walked into the forest, heading north once more.

"I love you Savannah Johnston," he shouted to the trees. "Someday I'll tell you the story of Moses and his family. Yes I will."

As the afternoon dwindled and that coveted sunshine had failed to materialize he saw something move in the trees just ahead of him. He dropped onto the ground, painfully aware that Bat's pot had rattled. He held his breath, daring not to move and staring at the spot of the movement. An animal he asked himself? A Rebel patrol? A fleeing slave as Moses and his family were? Then he saw movement again, but this time at ground level. Had someone seen him and dropped to the ground as he had? Was he being watched this very moment? Was someone aiming a gun in his direction?

Then he saw it. It moved and grew bigger; a man stood up and moved slowly toward Joshua. Joshua regretted not having a gun. He thought about running. Too late. He tried to bury himself in the loam; to get as hidden as possible. He cursed himself silently for his lack of awareness, for his imagining that Moses and that hint of sun-light had seemed a good omen and allowing himself the pleasure of drifting onward while dreaming of the time he would see Savannah again and how their life would be. In his imagination he had seen himself sitting with Savannah wrapped in his arms and telling her about his adventures while walking north. Telling her about Moses and his family and telling her about his first meeting with Sergeant Daniel Kelly and his Reunion with the soldiers of the 98th Pennsylvania Volunteers. He saw himself telling her about his experiences during the rest of the war and how his regiment had honored itself in battle after battle and how it had been chosen the Lincoln Brigade with full honors and recognition by Abraham Lincoln himself. He wanted to tell her how each surviving member of the Lincoln Brigade would have been presented with a signed copy of Lincoln's Gettysburg Address; that now celebrated speech given in November 1863 on the hallowed Battlefields of Gettysburg.

But that was all a dream; a hope for the future. The Honor Brigade was all in Joshua's imagination as he watched that ominous specter moving slowly toward him through the trees. Now it was clearly a man; a man in a shabby Confederate uniform. If he carried a weapon it was not visible.

He wore no leather that would conceal a revolver and his hands were free of a carbine or musket. He carried what looked like a bedroll and haversack, either could have concealed a weapon. Were there others? Joshua stood up. He knew it was not common for soldiers to conceal weapons in their haversacks or bedroll. But!

The Confederate came up within 30 feet of Joshua and stopped. He was thread bare; unshaven, dirty, skinny, and broken looking. Joshua discerned a hint of alarm in the eyes and at the corners of his bearded mouth. A butternut clad arm came up in a sign of amity. Joshua did not return the gesture but stood watching the every move and considering an escape route if things suddenly turned ugly. The arm and the shoulders bore no insignia of rank; a private at most. Joshua thought about the sleeve of his Union Army uniform bearing what was left of badly faded corporal's stripes. He stood there knowing full well he was facing the enemy. How to kill this man, was one of the myriad thoughts crowding into his consciousness. He glanced about for a weapon.

When the Confederate soldier was within 20 or so feet of Joshua he suddenly spoke. "Well, I seen ya'll. Ain't no sense in avoid' in me.

Joshua was now standing full upright. "Well I see you too," he said.

Silence. The soldier stopped and stood still and then dropped his bedroll and haversack onto the ground. He raised both hands as if in a sign of surrender. Joshua was cautious and dropped his bedroll to the ground in order to free his hands.

"You a yank?"

"Who in hell wants to know?" Joshua said.

"Me."

"You a Reb soldier?"

"Maybe I am and maybe I ain't…no more anyhow."

"Well?" Joshua said.

The soldier lowered his hands. "Oh hell…I'm a private in the 84th Alabamy. Or, I was anyway."

"Ya'll gonna want to kill me? Joshua said.

"Not unless I shoot ya'll with the gun I don't got."

"I don't neither," Joshua said, raising his empty hands.

"Hell, I ain't had a gun in ten days or more," the soldier said.

"You lost? Joshua said.

"Sort of."

"What ya mean…sort of?"

"Go 'in home to my fambly in Alabamy."

"With permission or without? Joshua said.

"Ah…not exactly with."

"You alone?"

"As a bobcat."

"You wanna talk a bit?"

"Cain't hurt."

They sat cautiously across a small brook from each other.

"What's your name?" the soldier said.

"Josh…Joshua Cole. You?"

"Abel Witherspoon."

"You a deserter? Joshua said.

"Guess I am," Abel said. "I've had enough of this here stink' in war.

Ya'll Yanks just kill' in people in order to free the niggers."

"Slaving ain't right," Joshua said.

"Who are you Yanks to decide right and wrong?"

Joshua grinned. "Because God is on our side."

Abel laughed. "Ha. Ya'll a corporal, huh?"

"Yes, and I ain't no deserter like you."

"Then what are ya?"

"Prisoner in your Andersonville Prison. Place not fit for dogs."

"You just make' in that up?" Abel said.

"Suit yourself," Joshua said. "I been there and I seen it and felt it."

"Yeah," Abel said, "then how'd ya git away?"

Joshua told him.

"I'll bet they shot that there guard that let ya'll run off," Abel said.

"Hope not," Joshua said. "But I can't figure him out."

"In truth, "Abel said, "he's probably as sick of the whole mess as you were."

Joshua got up and waded across the brook to Abel's side and sat down next to him. "You got any coffee or tea?"

Abel dug into his haversack. "Spoon full or two of coffee, but I ain't got no pot to cook it in."

Joshua filled Bat's kettle with water from the brook while Abel started a small fire with dry bark from the underside of a fallen tree. Twenty minutes later they were sipping a very weak coffee.

"You could read a newspaper through this stuff," Abel said, "so weak."

"First coffee I had in a long time," Joshua said. "Any coffee is better than no coffee."

"Ain't that right."

"Wish I had a cigar to smoke," Joshua said.

"Ya'll smoke cigars?"

"My first sergeant offered me one from time to time," Joshua said.

"My first sergeant would shoot me on sight if he could, "Abel said.

"Why'd you run off from your regiment?" Joshua said.

Abel sipped his coffee and seemed to think about an answer.

"Month or so ago we came across a battlefield that's more than a year or two old. Theys skeletons in the grass. Bone white skulls with hair still on them. Ain't nobody cares 'bout those there troops that died back then. Nobody cares. No one even bothered to bury them. Just let them rot there in the field so's the animals could feed off them and such. Theys dead and gone an theys fambly don't even know what's happened to them. So's I say to myself, Abel, git out 'a here. Go' wan home to your fambly 'cause this here war is a loss and ain't nobody cares 'bout those who died fighting it. So here I am drink' in coffee with a yank who's probably kilt some of my folks."

I hear ya Reb," Joshua said, "I seen rats eating off the dead at Andersonville Prison, cats too, and ain't nobody cared a might. Theys just ghosts of battles past."

"Well," Abel said, "I know I kilt some of your folks too, so we's even on that account. But all those dead have been gathered to their fathers so's it don't matter who's side they was on."

"You got a wife and children, Abel?"

"Maryanne and Meredith is their names. You, Joshua?"

"No wife but a girl I fell in love with. Aim to go back to her when the fighting is done."

"She in Pennsylvany?"

Joshua looked off into the trees. "Not exactly. She's a southern girl that helped me after escaping from that prison. You have good people here."

Abel looked at Joshua and shook his head. "Tell me it warn't no southern gal."

"Was, but she was just trying to help a…what did she call me, a stray pup. No harm in her do'in that."

"She helped a Yank? No sir, that ain't proper for a southern lady."

"Savannah is a great person and it ain't her fault I fell in love with her. She's the niece of your General Joe Johnston. I think he being a great soldier would be proud of her."

"He'd likely whup her butt if he knew. She a plantation belle? Likely a Johnston farm, hey? Savannah Johnston? That there plantation must be somewhere's down near Jeffersonville."

"Sounds right," Joshua said, "but I never got over near there. Too many ya'll Rebs in Jeffersonville."

Witherspoon was grinning. "You bed her a time or two?"

Joshua realized he'd already said too much. There was that persistent desire of his to talk about the girls he loved. In the past he'd bothered anyone that would listen about his love for Katie Hespeth.

"Forget it," Joshua said, "she did nothing but help another person."

"Well did ya?"

Joshua knew he needed to change the subject quickly. His mind raced.

"They'll shoot you ya know," Joshua said, "when the catch you."

"No they won't," Abel said, "cause this here War will be over and no one will care. But…Joshua…theys gonna shoot you 'cause ya'll gonna win this here war and the army ain't gonna take kindly to your lie about Andersonville Prison. Theys gonna say ya'll a deserter."

"Not my regiment," Joshua said. "They know my record in battle."

Joshua got up and threw the rest of his coffee on the fire.

"I ain't lying...I guess I'll be seeing ya," he said. He picked up his bedroll and the kettle and walked across the brook into the trees.

"No sir," Abel called after him, "I hope we won't be see' in each other."

"Good luck to you Reb," Joshua yelled. "And thanks for the coffee...such as it was."

Despite the disagreeableness of Abel Witherspoon Joshua felt a bit lonelier after walking away. Witherspoon was someone to talk to and was someone to rub shoulders with as they would say in the Union Army, brothers in arms walking shoulder to shoulder. Witherspoon was the enemy but he had been in the fight too and in a powerful sense that made he and Joshua brothers walking side by side through the same hellish experience.

That night Joshua camped near a brook and was able to catch a large catfish with a spear he'd fashioned out of a tree branch. He gutted the fish and skewered it over his small fire and ate head and all. That night laying wrapped in Savannah's blankets he felt sick and realized his stomach was not used to that much food all at once. Prior to dawn he vomited into the bushes several times before he could manage a resemblance of sleep.

The morning found him still nauseous and weak. Downcast, he walked on feeling himself nothing more than a little shadow on the earth, meaningless, and no more important than those killed in the war and laying now in their own decaying puddles of rotting flesh, forgotten for all time and amounting to nothing more that the discarded residue of war. He pictured himself dying alone someplace in these woods, his bones unfound and scattered by animals. Savannah would never know what happened to him and spend the rest of her life suspecting that their love had been a temporary romance inspired by the dregs of war and that he had abandoned her for 'that girl back home.'

The days that followed were hideously blurred by starvation and dread. Joshua seemed to congeal at night despite the console of Savannah's blankets and crawled out into the wraithlike mists of dawn each morning shaking and chilled and trying to stand on weakening knees and then guiding himself onward with eyes that seemed unable to focus. He felt lost continually and at times found himself stepping across his own shoe prints that he had created hours earlier. Each time that happened he knew that he was walking in circles. He had learned at Camp Curtain during training that men lost in the woods walked in circles, crossing and re-crossing their own trails until exhausted they died from exposure. His desire to give up and lay down and die infiltrated his thinking but then at crucial failing moments his desire to return and spend his life with Savannah took over and with strength arising from he knew not where, got back to his feet and walked on.

Two days after he left Witherspoon Joshua walked into the killing field Witherspoon had described. At first he thought it was just a grayish stone lying amid tall grass. Closer inspection turned it into a human skull with clumps of hair still attached. Near the skull human ribs protruded out of the loam like a grinning reminder of the bitter devastation of the dubious human spirit. Joshua strolled about the killing field in a trance. To date his experience with battle fields was the immediate aftermath; broken bodies, devastated equipment and wagons, burning debris, and the smell of the freshly dead.

But this scene was different, even different than the burying fields of Andersonville Prison. At Andersonville the dead had been buried, some of their remaining affects gathered for their families, if any, and final words said over their graves. In this killing field the dead had been lost for all eternity. Families would wonder down all the years; where did Henry go? What happened to him? Where is he buried? Will he return some day? Will he suddenly walk in? Did he suffer alone? And...I never new my dad...the lament of the young. Saved only for his returns to the fatherless in treasured final letters sent to the wife from some war-torn battlefield holding, perhaps, and often, a last poignant word to loved ones, or maybe by chance, a faded tintype that a widow held dear; a ring he left behind or an old hat in the attic that he had worn, sweated in and shaped, leaving the mark of a man that had been, but would be no more than a ghost of times past.

Joshua lingered amidst the dead thinking that he should say some words over these sun-bleached bones of humans that had once cherished dreams of the future; of a loved one at home; of a baby boy or girl, yet unseen. But he didn't say words, instead he shouldered his bedroll and walked on full of a new emptiness that haunted his soul and followed him on into another lonely night. In his restless dreams that night Savannah Johnston eluded him as he wondered through tall grass gathering human bones in haversacks and lamenting the devastation of the human soul.

CHAPTER TWENTY-TWO

Doubt

Eight days after meeting Abel Witherspoon Joshua heard a bugle call in the distance. He froze because he knew that sound, it was the call to arms, and hopefully, the Union Army. The call was music to his ears; a memorable sound he had not heard in months. At first he'd thought it was just his starving imagination but when the call echoed through the trees again, and then again, he suddenly felt ice-like chills run up and down his spine. Hope! Hope was in the offing. The rare possibility that it was his own regiment crossed his mind as he struggled through trees and brush toward the call, his legs failing and worsening with each anxious step. He hadn't eaten anything in two days and then only some dried corn kernels he'd found in a field near a burned out and abandoned farmstead. He'd ground the kernels between rocks, mixed the meal in water and eaten it cold, his matches and that simple pleasure of a nightly fire long past.

Half an hour later Joshua saw a very familiar sight; neat rows of white two-man tents spreading uniformly up a slope on the opposite side of a small stream. As he'd walked toward the camp other army sounds had begun to drift his way. It wasn't long before Joshua knew that somewhere just ahead was an army bivouac. Horses whinnied, pots tinkled, rattled and men's voices drifted faintly through the trees. The pleasant smell of wood smoke soon came to him and the thought of food and warmth crowded everything else out of his mind; his usual caution faded. He plunged across the creek and crept into a clump of low bushes to a spot where he could better observe the encampment and determine if they were friend or foe.

Soon the blue uniforms of the Union Army settled his mind on any questions he might have had about approaching the bivouac. Hurriedly he began moving toward the encampment and making purposeful noise in order to avoid being shot as a spying enemy or scout. Within his first hundred steps Joshua was abruptly confronted by a previously unseen picketing soldier who stepped out of the trees and quickly aimed his musket at Joshua, ordering him either to holt or be shot. Joshua raised his hands in surrender and sat down in the grass. He was saved. He failed to hold back the hot tears of joy.

"Yes siree I've heard that lie before," the picket said. "Ya'll just sit still whilst I call for some help and you can tell my sergeant that there lie about Andersonville Prison. Ya'll a deserter, no doubt about it."

Joshua struggled unsteadily to his feet. "Ain't no lie private. I'm Corporal Josh Cole, Company A, 98th Pennsylvania Volunteers and I been walking for weeks to get back to this here army. Now git off your high horse and get that sergeant here."

"What's ya'll's regiment? The picket asked, squinting and looking doubtful.

"I just told you, 98th Pennsylvania Volunteers, Colonel Pickens in command."

"I heard that some colonel named Pickens up north got his self-kilt."

"I hope you heard wrong," Joshua said.

"Fact is I heard that some Pennsylvanny outfit got overwhelmed by a whole Reb division. Left most them dead in the grass. What was left went to prisoners. Yes 'siree I do think, if I remember right, it was the 98th."

"You could be wrong," Joshua said, his stomach tightening into a hard knot.

"Well you volunteers are known for run' in off when the fight' in starts. That what you did?"

"I was wounded and captured and taken by train to Andersonville, Georgia and imprisoned. Open your God damned eyes and look at this scar on my forehead. Reb mini-ball done that."

Joshua exhausted from the effort sank back down to his knees.

"I heard that the on'y Reb prison was in Virginy somewhere. Libby Prison, or sum'thin like that."

"Get your sergeant. I need food. I sick. I'm not a deserter."

Half an hour later Joshua stood at attention as best he could on trembling legs in the entrance to an officer's tent and for the second or third time attempted to explain his whereabouts during the past few months. A colonel and a major sat behind a table. A provost sergeant stood at their side. The provost sergeant bore a small sneer on his bewhiskered face as Joshua spoke. The colonel was smoking a cigar. The aroma reminded Joshua of Sergeant Dan Kelly. Having found out that this huge encampment was a corps in General Meade's Army of the Potomac, Joshua sorrowfully realized that his own regiment, divisions and corps were somewhere in the north fighting the remnants of Lee's Army of Northern Virginia. He asked the colonel for any news he might have about the 98th Pennsylvania but was ignored.

"Well Corporal," the Colonel said, "I ain't too certain I believe this here story about Andersonville Prison. However,

I do know that such a prison exists down there. But in the meantime you are under arrest until we can sort this thing out. In the interim I'll send a rider up north and see what your commander has to say about you. However once again, the word down the line is that Colonel Pickens was kilt a month or two ago, so I really don't know who's in charge. Perhaps General Meade his self will have to hear you out. Sergeant Conner, confine the Corporal for now and see that he gets fed proper and have the medical officer check him over."

Then the colonel turned to the major. "Major, do you agree with this?" The major looked at Joshua for a long moment and then said, "You can shoot him right now far as I'm concerned."

"That is not in order," the colonel said. "Every man has a right to be heard."

Joshua was marched by the provost sergeant to a tent and put inside with a nasty admonition that should he step outside without permission he'd be shot on sight.

"You gotta piss," the provost said, "holler like hell until someone stands by."

More than two hours later a private arrived with a plate of salt pork, corn meal and hard tack biscuits. He was handed a canteen full of water and admonished to make it last. The medical officer never bothered to show up and eventually Joshua decided that it wasn't going to happen.

He'd hoped for some medical attention for wounds and the resulting infections he suffered along the way. His right knee was badly infected from a cut suffered when he'd fallen on a rock and there were a number of thorn scratches on his arms, legs and face that were red and swollen. He'd asked for coffee but the private had replied, "People in hell want cold water too, so don't hold your breath."

At sundown two more prisoners were deposited in the tent with Joshua. The were dirty, ragged and looked like they hadn't eaten in days. They came into the tent and avoided speaking to Joshua. The guards that brought them delivered three wool army blankets, a pot of stew, half a dozen hard tack biscuits, three bowls and tin cups. Both the new men huddled together in a corner sitting on their blankets, eating and talking between themselves. Joshua felt that he might as well have not been there.

"We gonna be shot God damn it," one said. "I told ya we shouldn't have run off. Now we's deserters and theys shoot 'in deserters just to set an example." Both turned and looked at Joshua but neither spoke.

"Oh shut up Freddie," the other said, "they ain't gonna shoot us. Hell we only been gone a week or 10 days. Ain't like we run off for good."

"Yeah, well it's like be 'in a woman swollen with child, you either pregnant or you ain't. We's deserters and that's a fact."

Joshua sat quietly on his blanket and listened. It was as if the other two hadn't noticed him. His food sat ignored for a time on a wooden platter before Joshua, while listening to the deserters debate their situation decided to eat alone. Both deserters looked up and frowned in unison.

"Don't eat it all," one of them said. "We ain't et much this past week."

"Shit," the other said, "we ain't et anything."

Joshua slid the platter toward the two men.

"Fact is," one said, "you look like you ain't et much in a month."

"I ain't," Joshua said. "I was a prisoner in Georgia, got away and walked north to find my regiment."

One of the men grinned. "Naw, ya'll a deserter just like us."

"They ain't gonna believe that bullshit about Andersonville Prison," the other one said.

"You ran like a rabbit when the shoot' in started, didn't ya? The first one said.

"And now you want' in to get back in good graces with the army and not have your ass shot off for desertion."

Joshua lay back on his blanket and ignored them. He would spend his time preparing his defense if, in fact, he was accused of desertion. And, he thought, that seems likely. Eventually he slept a restless kind of sleep and was irritatingly aware that throughout the night the other two were talking and arguing about their situation. It was clear they too were trying to come up with a reasonable defense for their absence. Twice during the night he asked them to be quiet and was met with disdain. Joshua even tried to use his rank to threaten them but once again was ridiculed.

"You ain't no corporal no more," one of the said, "Ya'll a jail bird just like us. You can take your corporal stripes and shove'im."

At dawn a private arrived at the tent with a bowl of hot corn meal and one cup of coffee. The coffee was cold. He gave Joshua the food and turned to leave. One of the other prisoners stopped him.

"Where in the hell's our breakfast?" he yelled.

The private did not turn around but left the tent.

"Hey horse's ass," the other yelled, "where's my grub?"

"Ya'll ain't gonna need no grub this morning," a voice came from outside the tent.

The two prisoners froze, staring at each other.

"What in the hell is that supposed to mean?" one said.

The other prisoner suddenly sat down on his blanket.

"Holy Mother of God," he said, "theys gonna shoot us this morning."

The other prisoner started pacing back and forth.

"We gotta run for it," he said.

"Cain't," the other one said, "theys that guard outside the tent."

"Well shit Freddie, theys gonna shoot us anyways."

Footsteps outside the tent. Leather squeaking. Whispering. The tent flap jerked open. The big provost sergeant leaned in and Joshua could see three or four soldiers just behind him. Each soldier had a rifle over his shoulder and two were carrying length of hemp rope.

The big sergeant came in and was handed the pieces of hemp. He ordered both prisoners to turn around and place their hands behind there backs. They complied and he tied there wrists tightly and then turned them and shoved them outside through the tent flap. Just outside the tent a commotion erupted.

"Sergeant Sir," Joshua heard one of the prisoners say, "ya'll ain't gonna shoot us are ya? Shit, we ain't dun nuthin bad."

"Shut your mouth," he heard the sergeant say, "ain't up to me."

"But Sergeant Sir, we ain't even had a trial. We ain't been heard."

"Tell the colonel your problems. Like I said, it ain't up to me."

"Well let me see the colonel then. For Christ sake, Sergeant."

Joshua looked out through the open flap. The sergeant stopped, turned around and grinned. "You'll see the colonel as he drops his saber and the boys open fire."

"For God's sake, Sergeant."

"Relax," the sergeant said, "you got time. Theys gonna make you dig your own graves before they shoot you. Maybe build the coffins."

"Well you go straight to hell Sergeant; I ain't digging no graves...specially my own."

"Up to you," the sergeant said. "They'll just shoot you all that much sooner."

Joshua heard shuffling footsteps as the assemblage marched away from the tent and then an appalling silence. The only sound in camp was the occasional snort of a horse or the tinkle of cooking ware. Joshua put his food down un-eaten. He couldn't eat. His stomach twisted and he lay back on his blanket waiting for the inevitable shots he knew would come soon. An endless hour passed before he heard them. They came as a volley followed by shuffling footsteps as the troops that had been assembled to witness the executions tramped away. Officers always required their troops to observe the executions believing it deterred desertion. There were no conversations between the departing troops with only the dismissal order from an officer to disperse echoing off the trees followed by a ominous silence through-out the camp. Watching a fellow soldier executed caused considerable bitterness throughout the units because there wasn't scarcely a soldier in the army who hadn't considered deserting at one time or another. Each soldier knew well the countless reasons a man might want to run away.

Two hours later Joshua heard pounding as the camp carpenter nailed the lids on two coffins accompanied by digging sounds nearby. That afternoon he was aware that the dead deserters were being buried when hearing the chaplain quietly reading psalms over the graves accompanied by shoveling noises and the familiar complaining by soldiers assigned an unpleasant task.

The following morning Joshua waited for something to eat but nothing came. He refused to complain about it not wanting to give his tormentors any satisfaction. For a time he thought that maybe they were going to shoot him but settled down some after the usual morning execution time had drifted past. The morning wore on and then just before noon his tent flap was thrown open and the same provost sergeant and two soldiers came in.

"Get your stuff together," the sergeant said, "you're leaving."

"What stuff, "Joshua said? "I'm wearing everything I own."

They marched him at gunpoint to a wagon hitched to a team of horses and sat him in the back with his hands tied in front. A driver climb aboard and urged the horses off. The two soldiers were mounted and followed closely behind the wagon.

Joshua leaned back against a side-rail. It was a warm morning and the sun peaked through trees along the way warming Joshua some but not doing much to relieve his hunger and thirst. An hour or so passed and he decided to talk to the driver.

"Ya'll mind telling me where I'm going?"

The driver turned and looked back at Joshua. "We're taking you back to your regiment so's they can shoot you and we won't have to."

"Where's my regiment?"

"Couple of days or three up north, up near the southern Blue Ridge or somewhere along there maybe Cedar Springs. Hell, I don't really know. We'll find'im. Theys sending an escort out to meet us. Theys take you on in."

"Who? Joshua asked.

"Ya'll's regiment. The 98th Pennsylvanny."

"Any chance I could have a drink of that water you got there in that canteen?"

"Ain't suppose to indulge a deserter but I guess it won't hurt."

"Forget the water," Joshua said, "I ain't a deserter. I was captured, imprisoned, and escaped. All's I want is to get back to my regiment and get on with the fight 'in."

"Suit yourself about the water," the driver said, "but your war is over. You'll get fed and watered at noon when we stop."

""You're go' in to a lot of trouble to get me home," Joshua said.

One of the escort riders yelled at Joshua to shut up.

"I ain't shutting up until I've been heard proper and the truth is settled on."

"You'll git your day in court," one of the riders yelled. Then they both laughed. "The 98th won't shoot you like those others without a trial."

The driver turned and suddenly tossed the canteen to Joshua.

"Have yourself a drink. I'm sorry for what I said about you be 'in a deserter. How in the hell would I know?" Then he tossed a haversack to Joshua. "There's some hard tack and salt pork in there. You might as well eat some."

Joshua looked at the haversack. "This your grub?"

"Enough for both of us," the driver said.

"What's your name?" Joshua said.

"Ernest Compton. They call me Ernie though."

"Well thank you Ernie for the water and food."

One of the riders shouted, "Both ya shut up. Ernie you ain't supposed to pal-up with the prisoner."

"Go to hell Carl," Ernest yelled.

"How long you been in the army?" Joshua said.

Ernest laughed. "Shit, since I was just a pup. I was a first sergeant once but that God damned demon rum ruined it all. Seventeen years in this God-awful army and I'm nothing but a fucking private...useless Waggoner."

Two hours later the wagon stopped and all took time to relieve themselves. One of the escorts stood right behind Joshua as he urinated.

"Don't you get any funny thoughts about running," he said.

Joshua stood by a tree and remembered how he had made a run for it at Andersonville and the thought crossed his mind that just maybe he should run for it now. But why? He wasn't a deserter and when he arrived back at the 98th Pennsylvania he would be welcomed with open arms and be able to spend days regaling Sergeant Kelly and others about his escape from Andersonville Prison and his travels north getting back to his army. He could even admit his love for Savannah Johnston because she had helped him along his way back north. He could tell them that she was not a Southerner but a very decent human being and viewed him as a person, as a man, and not a Yank nor enemy, and that she was very beautiful on top of it all. And he could tell them about Battis and how a black slave had given his life to protect a Yankee soldier. He could even tell them about his and Savannah's plans for after the war.

Joshua's reverie was broken by one of the escort riders.

"Git back in the wagon deserter," he yelled.

"Ernie," Joshua said, "do you think I could get these ropes of my hands? I ain't going anywhere. If I run it would look for sure like I was deserter."

"Climb up here on the seat beside me. Fuck those riders behind us. I'll take those ropes off' in ya."

"Ain't supposed to do it," one of the riders yelled.

Ernest ignored him and took out a wooden-handled knife and cut the ropes away from Joshua's wrists.

"Your responsibility," one of the riders yelled.

"Go to hell Carl," Ernest yelled, "he ain't go' in no where."

Joshua felt relief when he sensed an improved blood-flow into his hands. He rubbed them vigorously together, slapping them on the wagon seat for stimulation.

"Thank you Ernie," he said, "I won't let you down."

As they rode along Joshua began to feel a tingle of excitement in his stomach at the thought of being back with his regiment and seeing Sergeant Kelly again. Then the thought hit him that maybe Dan Kelly had been wounded in action, or maybe worse. He found himself looking forward to standing straight and saluting Colonel Pickens again, praying that the rumors of his death were just that, and rubbing elbows with those men he had been to war with creating a life-long bond. He imagined himself in a fresh uniform with a new set of colorful corporal's stripes on the sleeve and even allowed himself to imagine that maybe, just maybe, before the war was over he might sew a set of sergeant's stripes on those sleeves. He had even heard that sometimes sergeants were commissioned brevet lieutenants and became officers. Now wouldn't that be something, he thought. Imagine arriving back at Johnston Manor in a sparkling uniform with lieutenant's bars on his shoulders and his pockets full of back pay. There was even the possibility that Sergeant Dan Kelly had been commissioned a lieutenant by now. Kelly was certainly superior to a myriad of officers he'd known.

On this day he allowed himself to imagine that the possibilities for his future were endless. He began thinking about Savannah and their night of the rules and he thought about what he would give to hold her in his arms again. But then a certain fear knotted his stomach as he wondered if Savannah was okay. She was alone in a desolated country that was over-run with Rebel and Yank soldiers and lawless, murdering raiders.

The first night out two-man tents were put up with Joshua sharing one with Ernest Compton and the two guards sharing the other. One of the riders seemed to be in charge of the expedition and detailed picket duties between the three. Joshua was admonished not to get any ideas about running off during those times he was left alone. It seemed that by the end of the first day the three escorts were beginning to relax and even leaning in their discussions toward Joshua's possible innocence.

The days that followed wore on with the tedium of long hours in the sun and rain and cold damp nights beneath dripping canvas and the toxic monotony of the camp food consisting of salt pork, hard tack biscuits and coffee. The growing worry amongst the escorts was that they would be discovered by a roving Confederate cavalry or a band of Rebel militia-type raiders. It was well known that General Robert E. Lee had commissioned several groups of Rebel raiders who were governed by very little military obedience and whose sole duty was to harass the northern troops, capture wagon trains, and rob, murder and steal at will. The escorts had learned from civilians along the way that a group known as Mosby's Raiders were marauding and harassing in the rural areas all along the east side of the Blue Ridge Mountains and all the way up to Paris, Virginia and the Ashby Gap. There was a rumor that Mosby and his men had even ridden into Middleburg, Virginia during the night robbing and looting as they went and were only driven away by local word that a troop of Union Cavalry were riding hard in that direction. The only promising part of the rumor was that Mosby himself had been wounded in the raid. Joshua heard that some Folks were referring to Mosby as *the Gray Ghost*.

The afternoon of the eighth day out Joshua's awareness flared as a soothing thought crowded into his consciousness telling him that his 'people', and his army were very near.

CHAPTER TWENTY-THREE

Inquisition

"Smells like my regiment's fires," Joshua said to the wagoner.

"How would ya'll know? Ernest said. "One camp fire smells just like another."

"I can just tell," Joshua said.

"Well your regiment is a bunch of lazy asses," Ernest said, "they didn't bother to ride out to meet us. Too much God damned trouble, I guess."

"Could be they have better things to do," Joshua said.

"Halt right there, "a picket yelled. Two Union pickets aimed muskets at the wagon and the out-riders. Ernest pulled the horses to a stop and raised his hands. One of the escort riders informed the picket of the business at hand while the other urged his horse forward.

"Seventy-first New York," he said. "Were bringing in one of your deserters." Then he looked at Joshua and grinned. "But I don't think he really is one. Seems he could 'a run off any time along this here trip but he didn't."

"I'll walk you in," the picket said.

Joshua didn't recognize the picket, thinking he must be a replacement.

"I ain't coming in until you bring Colonel Pickens or Captain Reynolds out her so I can state my case."

"You been running for a while ain't ya, Corporal what's-your-name?"

"Get me the Colonel," Joshua demanded. "And it's Joshua Cole."

"Well shit Corporal I'd just loved to but he's just about five or six feet under at the moment."

"Kilt? "Joshua said.

"Yes sir," the picket said, "oh hell, more 'in a month ago, I guess."

"Captain Reynolds? Joshua said.

"Shipped up to Annapolis weeks ago. Got his leg blown off by a cannon ball. Yes sir he did, right at the knee."

"Sergeant Kelly? Joshua said. "Dan Kelly." Joshua felt some anxiety.

"Well ya'll got one there. Kelly's up there in camp. Hell nothing would kill that old bastard."

Joshua breathed easier with that news. Dan Kelly was alive and well.

"He ain't an old bastard and…go fetch him."

"You're kind of bossy for a deserter, ain't ya?"

"I ain't a deserter and I'm a corporal in this here regiment. Sergeant Kelly…get him now."

"First we'll lock your ass up and then maybe I'll tell Sergeant Kelly about ya. Or perhaps better, Colonel Stall."

Joshua gave up and climbed down off the wagon. "Well enough," he said. "Thank you Ernie for your kindness."

"Well good luck to you," Ernest said. "Write to me in the 71st New York when this is over."

"I will for sure do that," Joshua said.

"He'll be lucky if they don't shoot his ass first thing in the morning," one of the escort riders said, chuckling."

"Can ya'll feed us," the other rider said, "before we head back?"

"That's up to the quartermaster I reckon," the picket said.

Joshua was sitting alone in a tent with a provost guard stationed outside when the tent flap opened and Sergeant Dan Kelly came in. Joshua jumped to his feet and couldn't help but salute his friend.

Kelly saluted back. "You don't gotta salute me Corporal Cole," Kelly said, grinning. Then he reached inside his coat and produced two cigars. "You look like hell," he said as he lit both cigars and handed one to Joshua. "And skinny. I'll bet I could see clean through ya on a bright day."

Joshua took Kelly's out-stretched right hand.

"Sergeant Kelly it is good to see you and be back with this regiment."

"You've got some catching up to do" Kelly said. "I guess you might have heard we lost Colonel Pickens some time ago. One hell of a fire-fight was on when he took a bullet in the head and fell off his horse. We found 4 bullet holes in his coat and one in his boot. He was dead when he hit the ground. He died sort 'a like General John Reynolds did up there at Gettysburg. Our Colonel Pickens was all man."

"And the Captain?" Joshua asked.

"Lost a leg. Cannon ball. Near died but we got him out of here soon enough…I think. Surgeon took what was left of his leg off right there in an old farm house we'd commandeered. They were both good men. Our big loss."

"I'm glad to have you back. What happened that day after the battle in camp?"

Joshua showed Kelly the scar from his head wound and explained that when he had recovered from being knocked unconscious he was a prisoner of the Rebs. He explained the burying of the dead and the horrific train trip to Andersonville, Georgia and his eventual escape and the history of this trip north. He told Kelly about how the Andersonville colonel had executed the 98th Pennsylvania soldiers by hanging and shooting without a proper trial or any mercy or justice whatever. He included the story about Johnston Manor, Savannah, and the death of Bat.

"I'm proud of you for making your way back north and I have to give that southern girl credit for hiding and helping a Yank. And it's too bad that slave fella, what was his name, Bat? Had to give his life to protect you. That's a story worth writing up someday."

"Maybe they'll come a time when I could," Joshua said. "After this war is finished I'm heading back south to my beautiful Savannah."

"Fell in love with that Reb girl" Kelly teased.

"I want 'a die in her arms," Joshua said.

"Well before you can die in her arms, Corporal Cole, you've gotta explain to the new colonel where you been for several months. Wouldn't be a problem at all if Colonel Pickens was still alive…or even Captain Reynolds was still here. This new crew of officers…well, I just don't know."

"And Captain Reynolds is gone for sure?" Joshua said.

"Gone for good I'm afraid," Kelly said. "We got a telegram that the infection kilt him a couple of weeks ago. Yes, it's for sure. No doubt at all. Things have changed here in the regiment. As you remember Major Barnes was kilt in that same battle that kilt Corporal Homan so we been without a major for quite some time. Colonel Stall is a bit difficult to git along with and the new captain ain't much better. However, I don't think there's much of a problem. Just about everyone these days has learnt about that Andersonville Prison down there in Georgia. Your inquiry should be pretty much routine. I'll have you back in the line in a week or less. You and I'll git this here war wrapped up soon and then you can go running back to that Southern Belle of yours."

"Can't be too soon," Joshua said. "I need to write to her. Can you arrange it?"

They sat quietly for a long time smoking their cigars before Kelly spoke again. "I'll come forward for you at the inquiry. You'll need to be as honest as Ole' Abe himself and tell the truth, including the help you got from Savannah Johnston and that slave fella. I think Colonel Stall will be amenable to your conduct on your way back north. You'll need to put some emphasis on your sickness after leaving the prison. It'll kind 'a explain why you stayed so long with Savannah Johnston…and of all the folks you'd tie up with…General Joe Johnston's niece. For God's sake Joshua. But right now I've got to deal with a couple Rebs we captured just this morning. I think they're deserters but ain't sure. I'll be back and eat some dinner with you at sun-down."

Kelly handed Joshua another cigar and a few matches and went out.

"I'll send you that letter writing stuff," Kelly said.

Early the following morning Joshua stood at attention in front of Colonel Stall and a Captain named Hershey. The colonel sat behind a broad table And the new captain and a lieutenant sat off to his left. A provost sergeant stood nearby with two armed soldiers. The colonel told Joshua to sit down. Joshua was garbed in a new uniform with bright yellow corporal stripes. His new brogans hurt. Two letters were secured inside his sack coat; One to his mother and the other to Katie Hespeth. The Hespeth letter had been very difficult to write. Explaining his feelings for Savannah Johnston and how their love had grown and how he planned to return to her after the war had been painful. Now, in conflict with his past worries about Katie, he hoped she had found a new love during his absence.

Sergeant Dan Kelly sat on a wooden bench to his right. Joshua saw a Confederate prisoner in a badly worn and frayed butternut uniform sitting off to one side with an armed guard. The Rebel soldier looked familiar but Joshua couldn't remember why. Perhaps the Reb had been one of the guards at Andersonville Prison. Wouldn't that be a generous turn of events? he thought.

An hour later Joshua had told the story of his wound, the train trip to Andersonville Prison, his escape and the walk north. The captain repeatedly questioned him about his stay at Johnston Manor and so much as accusing him of staying at Johnston Manor much longer than needed due to his infatuation with this 'Southern Belle'. The colonel sat nodding in agreement each time the captain pushed his points about Joshua's so-called 'dalliance' in the south. A new second lieutenant was assigned to defend Joshua but in all appearances he was intimidated by Colonel Stall and the captain and offered little defense.

The captain looked at the colonel and grinned. Obviously he was enjoying the interrogation.

"Now tell me Corporal Cole what those southern belles are really like. Ya know I heard all the rumors about theys penchant for passion...if you know what I mean."

Joshua stood up. "Go to hell, Captain."

Dan Kelly drew in a quick breath. "Corporal Cole," he admonished, "Sit down and be quiet."

The captain looked at Dan Kelly. "Silence, Sergeant Kelly. You haven't been called on yet."

"I'm ready," Kelly said, "...Captain Sir...your honor."

The captain scowled at Kelly. "Take the chair and let's hear what you've got to say about Corporal Cole here."

Kelly got up and went to the witness chair. He looked resplendent in his best uniform, his sergeant stripes fresh and colorful and his boots shined to perfection. He removed his cap and loosened two or three months' worth of coal black waves and curls. He was clean shaved, serving to accent his thick drooping mustache. He carried a stern countenance as he sat; one close to fierceness. Sergeant Dan Kelly was angry and it showed.

"To begin with," Kelly said," this here is a punitive court. You ain't look' in careful at the facts."

The captain slammed his fist onto the table and jumped up.

"Sergeant Kelly it is not your place to criticize this court. If you have something to say in favor of Corporal Cole then say it and be done. Anymore criticism from you and I'll dismiss you from this hearing."

Kelly nodded while staring straight into the eyes of the captain. The captain broke and looked away. Kelly smiled.

"Well I will repeat what I said…in a sense at least. Corporal Cole should not be sitting here on trial. I have personally been by his side in battle and he is one of the best troops I've ever supervised. He is brave under fire and I've never seen him even flinch when men are dying and falling around him and the God damned cannon balls are bouncing, killing and exploding. I wish I had a hundred just like him. This man should be a sergeant…no…a lieutenant. I want him back in the line and I want him promoted to sergeant so's I can get some decent help with these here troops. This man is a born leader and he needs to be congratulated for his escape from Andersonville Prison and his determination to come back north and join this here army. The man was sick and had been horribly abused in that prison and if some southern girl…bless her heart…found enough kindness to nurse him back to health, then we need to

respect and honor her also. God bless Savannah Johnston...
even if she is the niece of General Joe Johnston."

"Anything else?" the captain said.

"Yes...if this court finds Corporal Cole guilty of desertion
I'll lose any respect I ever had for this army and its body of
officers."

"Sergeant Kelly," Colonel Stall admonished, "you are out of
line again."

Joshua turned to Kelly. "Sergeant Kelly, don't."

"You finished sergeantKelly?" the captain said.

"I suppose," Kelly said.

"Next witness," the captain said, grinning.

Then the lightning struck. The Rebel prisoner swore to tell
the truth and took a bench near the colonel. That was when
Joshua recognized him. Abel Witherspoon nodded at Joshua
and smiled. Suddenly Joshua felt a growing fear in the pit of his
stomach. What was Witherspoon going to testify about? What
was he going to say? All kinds of possibilities flooded Joshua's
mind. Witherspoon is a prisoner, is he going to say whatever
they want him to say in order to gain favor with his captors.
Joshua now regretted having ever spent time with Witherspoon
and especially telling him about his love for Savannah.

"Private Witherspoon," the captain said," would you under
oath tell us about your meeting with Corporal Cole here, in
the woods, some time ago?"

Witherspoon looked at Joshua, but wouldn't hold eye-
contact. Joshua shook his head.

"Well, Captain Sir, I met Corporal Cole in the woods some
where's near Jeffersonville, I think it was, and we shared some
coffee and biscuits and a fire. Corporal Cole told me that he
spent a goodly amount of time with a southern girl on some

plantation and that they went and gone and fell in love and he was damned reluctant to leave her…as I would 'a been. And he said he was for sure going back to that there girl soon as he could…that is if he'd ever leave her in the first place."

The captain grinned. "Seems Corporal Cole spent a lot of time socializing with the enemy. Did he tell you he was, you know, intimate with this southern Belle?"

Witherspoon looked at Joshua and then away. "Oh yes sir he did. Fact is he told me all about it. He warn't bashful at all about it. He was mostly worried that he might' a got her with child."

The captain looked at the colonel and smiled. Then he looked at Joshua and shook his head.

"Shame on you Corporal Cole. Sleep' in with the enemy."

"That's a lie," Joshua said. "You can't believe a Confederate deserter."

"We're looking at all the facts," the colonel said. "Private Witherspoon has firsthand information that we need. I see no reason for him to lie about you and that girl. Seems you might have talked a little too much about your love-life, Corporal Cole."

"He has a good reason to lie," Joshua said, "he's your prisoner and wants your consideration. And you know that."

Witherspoon looked at Joshua and then looked away. Witherspoon was dismissed after the captain questioned him briefly about what he had said. Nothing changed. Joshua looked at Witherspoon and shook his head. Witherspoon would not look at him. A guard took Witherspoon away. He looked back at Joshua as he was led away and hung his head.

Sergeant Kelly asked to speak again. He repeated about Joshua's fearlessness in battle and told about the promotion and how it had been eagerly approved by the officers. The captain and colonel both appeared to be ignoring him while shuffling papers and lighting cigars. Kelly recounted the battle where Joshua was wounded and how the Union troops had abandoned their camp in the midst of a surprise attack by Confederates and had retreated into the forest where they eventually forged a river and regrouped miles away. He and his officers had been very aware that they had left wounded and dead troops behind. Kelly testified that it was a black mark on his military career and his sense of self and one that would never happen again, saying he would rather die in battle than be shamed again by being routed by the enemy. "I'll carry that shame to my death-bed," he said.

Colonel Stall puffed on his cigar and sat staring at Joshua. The captain and the lieutenant sat smiling in unison. Finally Colonel Stall got up and leaned against the table.

The atmosphere in the camp grew tediously hushed. Somewhere a horse or mule snorted. The wind high up in the trees the only murmur.

Joshua took a deep breath and looked at Dan Kelly. Kelly was staring at the Colonel with a threatening glower in his eyes. He looked ready to spring on the Colonel. Kelly was shaking his head no. The Colonel was smiling, obviously enjoying his power over these proceedings and people.

"I believe that the captain and the lieutenant will agree with my decision. In light of Corporal Cole's reluctance to return to this army immediately after his 'so-called' escape from Andersonville Prison and his subsequent bivouac with this southern belle, the enemy of the North, I believe whole heartedly and convincingly, that Corporal Cole is a deserter. Does the captain and the lieutenant agree with my thinking?"

They both nodded in agreement. Both smiling.

"Therefore by the powers invested in me I sentence you, Corporal Joshua David Cole, to be shot at sunrise tomorrow morning. This court martial is adjourned,"

Sergeant Daniel Kelly jumped to his feet.

"In all due respect Colonel that sentence is plain old bullshit. This man is a true Yankee soldier and he is a warrior in every part of his being. And you need approval from Abe Lincoln for this. That's the rule."

The Colonel took the cigar out of his mouth and turned to Sergeant Kelly.

"Sergeant Kelly I'll have you arrested if you say one more word. And, furthermore this is an emergency. I ain't got time for Lincoln's weep 'in sentiments. No sir, this execution will go as I directed."

Kelly raised his fist in anger. "The hell you'll have me arrested," he yelled. Kelly had acquired a revolver somewhere and he had it strapped to his waist. He stood up and rested his right hand on the butt of the gun. Colonel Stall appeared to look around for support. There was none. The captain and the lieutenant seemed to remove themselves emotionally from the incident. Neither looked toward the Colonel or Dan Kelly. A murmur arose front the troops. A voice somewhere in the back of the formation yelled "Kelly, Kelly…Sergeant Kelly. Then others began yelling Kelly.

Colonel Stall turned to the sergeant of the guard and nodded. The sergeant looked at Dan Kelly and then back at the colonel. He hesitated.

"Well? The colonel said.

"But sir?" the sergeant blurted out.

The Kelly chant turned into an angry grouse. Dan Kelly stood with is hand on the gun, smiling lightly around his mustache. He turned slightly and nodded toward the formation. Colonel Stall's face tightened, exhibiting the strained facial appearances of rout.

A voice coming from the back of the formation shouted.

"You arrest Sergeant Kelly and we'll shoot your ass."

The captain jumped to his feet.

"Who said that? Who in the hell said that?" Then numerous voices erupted in unison. First slowly and quietly and then in full voice.

"I did." Others yelled "We did."

"I hear that again I'll have someone shot," the Colonel yelled.

Dan Kelly angered, turned and walked away, then suddenly came back glaring at the officers and yelled, "Created by the hand of God...destroyed by the Hand of Man. God won't forgive you for this...and neither will I. And neither will Abraham Lincoln. I'll testify to that. Yes I will."

The sergeant looked at the colonel. The colonel nodded his head. "Forget it," he said. Relief spread across the sergeant's face.

The Colonel turned to the captain. "Captain, dismiss the troops."

"Right away, Sir," the Captain shouted, relief in his voice.

Then it started quietly somewhere in the back of the formation of soldiers. First one voice low and quiet but the singer unseen. The Colonel and Captain both stood up to survey the column. Then another voice chimed in low and gentle. Then another and another and then several voices and then many in chorus...Mine eyes have seen the glory of the coming of the Lord;

He is trampling out the vintage where the grapes of wrath Are stored...

The colonel clinched his jaw. "Captain, dismiss these men...now. The singing continued as the troops dispersed.

He hath loosed the fateful lightening of His terrible swift sword...

His truth is marching on...

CHAPTER TWENTY-FOUR

The Last Day

He heard a bird chirp. It was his first awareness that morning had come. He'd been awake all night. When the bird chirped he turned to his side and saw a blurred lightness coming through the wall of the tent. He nodded toward the dawn. Joshua had spent the night talking to Savannah and hoping that somehow she was hearing him, or was at least aware that he was there in her presences; hopefully somewhere in the shadows of her bedroom. He'd pretended that he was with her in bed, and that he was holding her and he hoped that somehow she knew; in some way knew he was there with her. He told her what had happened and that now he regretted leaving her, regretted his desire to return to the army and finish out the war as a good and loyal Union soldier. Now he knew that it had been a blunder, an error to think he would be welcomed with open arms and that his commanders would not be suspicious of his long absence. Now a fatal mistake. He sat very still for long time thinking about the past few months of his life. Once again he could see Bat's grave and how it had sunk in the rain and he could smell the pine sap and see it dripping down the sides of the coffin and he could see Savannah's bouquet wilted and laying over on the grave and he could see Savannah weeping quietly in the rain and he remembered how she had said that she was frightened because she saw herself dead in the rain. Then his senses startled him because he was sure he could smell the scent of lilacs. Was Savannah there? Had she come to him? No she hadn't. Joshua knew that this experience was his emotions working on him…working against him. Savannah was home on the plantation and waiting for his return. He could visualize her going each day to the little wooden bridge and looking up the road hoping to see him or her father returning. But then he would perceive her eventually turn and walk alone back to the manor house. He hated the thought of her lonely nights and he hated the fear he felt for her alone in that war-torn land.

He got up off his blankets and went to the water bucket and washed his face and hands. He could hear the morning sounds of the camp; men talking, breakfast fires crackling, eating utensil clinking and the occasional snort of a horse or mule. He missed the camp mornings. He wished he was out there with his troops talking and joking and with the smell of the bacon frying and the coffee brewing over the fires. And… he knew that some of these same men would be assigned within the hour to load their rifles and prepare themselves for an execution. And…he knew they would not like it…and that most would protest…and…be threatened with arrest for their 'audacity'. Some of them would defer, preferring the arrest, punishment and the ensuing consequences.

His tent flap opened and Dan Kelly came in with a coffee pot and two tin cups. He clearly looked tired. His huge mustache was askew and uncombed. He hadn't shaved. He wore only his boots, trousers, his kepi and a frayed and badly stained shirt that had once been white. Without speaking he sat down on the blankets and tapped a spot beside him for Joshua to sit on. Joshua sat down. Kelly poured two cups of coffee and then lit two cigars. They sat there without speaking sipping the hot coffee and smoking the cigars. Then Kelly abruptly threw his coffee and cigar into a corner off the tent, yelled "son-of-a-bitch," laid his hand on Joshua's shoulder, paused, turned and went out. Joshua thought he saw moisture in Dan Kelly's eyes. The core of the tent suddenly turned frigid. They came for him within the hour.

They sat him on a freshly built pine coffin. It was so fresh that Joshua could smell the pine sap as it ran down the sides in rivulets. It reminded him of something and then again he remembered Bat's pine coffin, the one he'd built the morning before they buried Bat. They wanted to blindfold him. He refused, saying he wanted to look his executioners in the eye. He wanted Colonel Stall to break and look away. He wanted the captain's stomach to crawl. He convinced them not to tie his hands. The firing squad was lined up 15 yards or so from him. The twelve soldiers looked grim. Joshua felt sorry for them. He could guess that at least two of them had not put balls in their muskets. And he knew that if they were caught doing that they would be severely punished. They were being forced to shoot one of their own. Probably one that was not a deserter as accused by an over-bearing and self-important colonel. Sergeant Kelly had told Joshua all about the failings of Colonel Stall. He was the same colonel that had stood back on a safe hillside watching the last battle through field glasses. The same colonel who refused to charge into a conflict alongside his troops. The same colonel who refused to tour a battle field after the smoke had cleared, apparently too terrified to come face to face with the carnage.

Joshua looked around at his soldier friends. So many of these men had become his brothers in arms. His brothers in death and destruction.

That same colonel now stood off to the side of the firing squad with his saber resting erect against his right shoulder. The squad had been given the command to aim their rifles. What was left of the Pennsylvania Ninety-eighth Regiment was formed up in neat rows having been ordered to witness the execution of a 'deserter', the common practice designed to discourage further absconding. The red, white and blue of the United States flag fluttered nearby in a soft morning breeze coming up the hill-side off of the gurgling creek a hundred or so yards away. The Company guidon fluttered gently to the left of the U.S. flag. Joshua smiled at the guidon. He had always loved that flag and had volunteered to carry it into battle on more than one occasion, knowing full well that the soldier who carried the guidon was the number one target of the enemy. The guidon carrier was nearly always the first soldier to fall in any battle.

Joshua asked to speak. The colonel nodded in agreement.

Joshua looked away from the officers and directly at Daniel Kelly.

"As my first sergeant has testified, I am not a deserter. Sergeant Kelly is a man I would willingly ride into Hell with. His word is golden, but you, my condemners, refuse to accept his word. So be it. I am not a deserter. I am a corporal in Company A, of the Ninety-eighth Pennsylvania Volunteers and I shall die so. I love my regiment, it is the officers I distain. Now it is time for you to have your pint of blood."

Joshua looked up at the sky and could see that it was going to be a clear cloudless day with just a hint of breeze in the tree tops. Then he saw an eagle soaring above the trees on its morning hunt for food.

"It is a sad fellow who dies without ever having seen an eagle soar," he said aloud.

The Colonel turned toward Joshua. "What?"

Joshua ignored him.

Then Sergeant Dan Kelly stepped out of the formation, walked to the Colonel and spit into the dirt in front of the boots. The Colonel looked down at the spittle. He stood there glaring at Kelly, his saber still on his shoulder. The firing squad lowered their muskets without having been told to do so. A murmur arose from the regiment.

"Yes, Sergeant Kelly?"

Kelly spit in the dirt again. "Colonel Stall I've an idea."

"Yes Sergeant Kelly?"

Kelly turned and pointed toward the snag of a fifty foot dead pine tree.

"Colonel there's a set of cross limbs on that there tree over there and it looks just like the Cross of the Crucifixion. Why don't you just nail the Corporal up there and crucify him just like the Romans did to Jesus? After all the corporal's initials are J.C."

The Colonel glared and pointed his saber at Kelly. "Lieutenant, arrest Sergeant Kelly."

The young lieutenant looked startled. "Sir ?"

"Arrest him now," the Colonel yelled.

Kelly rested his hand on the butt of the revolver now stuck in his belt. The young lieutenant hesitated and looked questioningly at the colonel.

"Now," the Colonel yelled.

Kelly took his hand off the butt of his pistol. "I won't shoot a pup like you," he said softly.

The young lieutenant looked relieved and gently took Kelly by the arm. Kelly shook the hand off and nodded threateningly.

"Hands off me you little pup," he said.

"That's' insubordination," the Colonel yelled. "I may have to shoot you after all, Sergeant Kelly."

Kelly smiled at him and nodded his disagreement.

A voice from the back of the formation yelled. "It's your ass, Colonel."

Another voice. "You gonna git your ass shot off."

A low murmur evolved from the lined-up troops. Colonel Stall looked at the troops, cast his eyes down and then returned the saber to his shoulder and nodded upwards. The firing squad returned their muskets to the aiming position. Sergeant Kelly walked away amongst the tents with the young lieutenant trailing behind like a frightened puppy.

That voice came again from the rear of the troops.

"You ain't gonna do nuthin to Sergeant Kelly. Do...it's your ass."

Another voice spoke up. "You won't like having a bullet up your ass."

The colonel ignored them.

"Ready," he yelled.

The firing squad cocked their muskets.

Joshua saw Savannah standing amongst the trees. He blinked and she was gone. "Come back," he said aloud. Then he thought he could smell Lilacs. She was there somewhere. "Come back," he said again. Then he thought he heard her voice. She was saying something, was it? "Please don't go." He listened for her voice to come again but only the wind high up in the tree tops spoke to him. Was it her voice on the wind? Then he heard her again.

"Joshua, please don't leave us."

Joshua was confused. He listened for her again. Now only the wind.

"Us?" he said aloud. "Us?"

Joshua looked up into the clear blue windless sky. The eagle was still there gliding on the wind, his wings spread wide.

"I have to go," he said aloud, "but my darling Savannah I will come every night and keep you warm and safe. I know love now because I have known you."

Then somewhere off in the distance Joshua thought he could hear singing. Yes it was singing. It was Moses and Isabella and Mavis...

"Swing low sweet chariot
a coming for to carry me home...
swing low..."

CHAPTER TWENTY-FIVE

Aftermath

Two years after Lee surrendered at Appomattox Joshua's mother had his body exhumed and reburied on the family farm near Hanover, Pennsylvania. Daniel Kelly attended the internment. The tombstone is still there to this day. Katie Hespeth eventually married and bore seven children and enjoyed five grandchildren. Sergeant Daniel Kelly resigned from the army after the war and two years later was elected sheriff of York County, Pennsylvania. He was murdered in the line of duty by a drunken soldier during his second term. He is buried in Arlington National Cemetery. Colonel Hector Johnston was killed at Petersburg, Virginia near the end of the war. Savannah Johnston remained on the plantation the remainder of her life. She never married. Her son was born several months after Joshua left. She named him Joshua David. Savannah passed away in 1912 during a rain storm. Joshua Johnston attended the Virginia Military Institute and was commissioned a first lieutenant in the United States Army. He served as a full colonel under Black Jack Pershing in World War One. He was listed as missing in action during the Muese-Argonne Offensive in France. His body was never found. And so it goes.